THE TOUCH OF SNOW

A GLACIAL BLOOD SERIES NOVEL

Anna Edwards

*Dear Emma,
family isnt always blood !
Anna Edwards*

Copyright © 2017 by Anna Edwards

All rights reserved. No part of this publication may be reproduced, distributed or transmitted in any form or by any means, without prior written permission.

www.AuthorAnnaEdwards.com

This is a work of fiction. Names, characters, places, and incidents are a product of the author's imagination. Locales and public names are sometimes used for atmospheric purposes. Any resemblance to actual people, living or dead, or to businesses, companies, events, institutions, or locales is completely coincidental.

Warning: This book contains sexually explicit scenes and adult language and may be considered offensive to some readers. This book is for sale to adults only, as defined by the laws of the country in which you made your purchase.

In addition, this book may contain content which could cause triggers to certain readers. You read at your own discretion.

Disclaimer: Please do not try any sexual practice, without the guidance of an experienced practitioner. Neither the publisher nor the author will be responsible for any loss, harm, injury or death resulting from the use of the information contained in this book.

Cover Design by www.CharityHendry.com
Logo Design by Charity Hendry
1st Editing by Dayna Hart, Hart to Heart Edits
2nd Editing by Heather Guimond
Formatting by Charity Hendry

The Touch of Snow/ Anna Edwards – 2nd ed.
ISBN 978-1548135140

Dedication –

To anyone that is different from what the norm is.
You are unique.
That is your power.

Acknowledgements:

Firstly, and always to my great friend Charity Hendry for always being there for me. For entertaining my crazy ideas and helping me bring them to fruition. Love you to bits.

I want to give special thanks to Heather Guimond of AFWB who helped me no end in getting this book into order after a difficult time. You really gave me my confidence back.

To my street team, Becca, Susan and Sheena. Thank you so much for all your fabulous posts.

To my beta's, who all really embraced this story from the start. Thank you Maggie, Michelle, Maria, Becca and Barb.

To my team of ARC readers, many that have been there with me since the beginning, especially Tanaka, Becky (looking forward to coffee), Chrystal, Teresa, Jessica and Sandra.

To Yvonne and the Heart of Steel Crew for hosting the release party.

To my family, thank you for all the support that you give me. Especially my children who helped me decide what shifting animals to have. Kas for my little boy and Brayden for my cat obsessed princess. You're still not reading mummy's books until you are eighteen though.

Finally, most importantly, to all the readers that have embraced me as an author. I'm so glad that you enjoy the stories that my mind creates. I hope I'm able to give you many more years of pleasure.

CONTENTS

PROLOGUE — 1
CHAPTER ONE — 2
CHAPTER TWO — 11
CHAPTER THREE — 21
CHAPTER FOUR — 29
CHAPTER FIVE — 36
CHAPTER SIX — 44
CHAPTER SEVEN — 51
CHAPTER EIGHT — 57
CHAPTER NINE — 64
CHAPTER TEN — 70
CHAPTER ELEVEN — 75
CHAPTER TWELVE — 82
CHAPTER THIRTEEN — 89
CHAPTER FOURTEEN — 97
CHAPTER FIFTEEN — 104
CHAPTER SIXTEEN — 111
CHAPTER SEVENTEEN — 118
CHAPTER EIGHTEEN — 124
CHAPTER NINETEEN — 130
EPILOGUE — 137
BOOKS BY ANNA EDWARDS — 141
DEAR READER — 142
PREVIEW OF CONTROLLING HERITAGE — 143
ABOUT ANNA EDWARDS — 146
CONNECT WITH ANNA EDWARDS — 147

PROLOGUE

They have been by our side for millennia, but very few humans know they exist. Through the ages legends and myths arose of werewolves, the like, powerful witches who could look into the future and possess the spirit of a man. The ancient Egyptians worshiped gods such as Anubis, Horus, and Isis.

In truth, these creatures are the link between animals and humans. They are able to shift between their human and animal form at will - only ever to the one animal though. What if shifters existed who could become anything they wanted?

What would someone be willing to do to possess that power? The power to be any animal with only a thought.

CHAPTER ONE

The barren desert wasteland with its hues of gold, orange, and red sped past the car window. The rock formations were a testament to years of erosion beaten down by forces greater than he could understand. As a shape-shifting snow leopard, Brayden Dillon knew a lot about the ways of Mother Nature. Considering he spent most of his time exploring the snow-capped peaks of The Glacial National Park he already had the air-conditioning turned up as high as it would go. The brand-new Ford Mustang he drove had been a gift from his Alpha, Kas, in recognition for a job done well. So was the break from duties as pack Enforcer. Why his mother had to live just outside Death Valley was beyond him. You really couldn't get a hotter place on Earth. She'd told him it was because his father had always lived in the snow. When he died, she decided to get some sun. She hadn't looked back.

He pulled his Mustang up outside the café and shut off the roar of the high-powered engine. The disapproving looks from the locals soon vanished when he climbed out of the car. His height of six foot five silenced any potential disagreement. He purred to himself in contentment, but that was quickly lost when the heat of the midday sun hit him. He was not designed for this weather. He had all the usual snow leopard attributes: thick black hair with smoky gray flecks, small ears, and big feet that helped with balance. He was pale because he rarely spent time sunbathing like the lions and tigers in his pack. Dusk to dawn was when he was the most active. He made quick steps towards the café and into the air-conditioned building.

He didn't see his mother, only a fresh-faced waitress. She wore the café's uniform--a barely-there skirt and a tank top that was almost a second skin. She was pretty, in a timid sort of way. Every time someone came near her she flinched, and he could smell her fear. Well, he assumed it was fear. His judgment was slightly clouded by the fact that he needed a drink, preferably ice cold and dumped over his head. She approached the seat he had taken near the counter.

"Hi. Welcome to the Last Stop. I'm Selene, and I'll be your waitress today. Can I get you an ice water to start with? It sure is a hot one out there today." Any sign of her nerves had disappeared, replaced with a business-like smile.

"Yes please, lots of ice. In fact, just bring me a big bowl of ice."

She laughed, her tiny nose crinkling up and dimples appearing in her cheeks. Up close, she was even prettier than he'd originally thought. "Let me guess." She took a step back and looked him up and down. "Well, the fact you seem as if you're melting, I take it you're not a southerner. The lack of a tan confirms that but I can't quite place the accent?"

"Montana."

"No wonder you're hot. I'll bring you ice cream as well." She spun around in her little ballet pumps and started to stride off. Something stopped her. She turned back and took another long look at him; an eyebrow raising in question.

"Brayden?"

"Yes." His reply was tentative. Not many people knew who he was. It was his job to be secretive and stay in the shadows.

"Your mother said you were coming. She had to go to a meeting in Pahrump. She should be back soon, but she said that you could go up to the apartment if you wanted. My God, now I really look at you, you look like the pictures she has of your father. God rest his soul." She bowed her head. Brayden couldn't help feel a little unease. This girl-- she couldn't have been more than eighteen from the looks of her--knew far too much about him. He just hoped she didn't know everything. His mother would never tell her that would she? "You head on up. I'll get your water, ice cubes, and ice cream, and bring it to you. It's my lunch break, I'll keep you company till she gets here."

He did as instructed. Mainly because he was freaked out by the insistent waitress, but also because his mother had the biggest freezer known to man. If he didn't get cold air on him soon, he was going to dissolve into a pile of fur on the floor.

His mother's apartment hadn't changed one bit from when he visited last year. It was decorated in a minimal style with clean lines and equally clean surfaces. She had always liked the latest trends in interior design. It had apparently annoyed his father to no end because he preferred to take things as they came, which in his case, was usually wild and chaotic. While he waited for Selene, Brayden opened the freezer and stuck his head in it. The blast of icy, cold air surrounded him, and his inner beast jumped for joy at finally getting away from the inferno that was the Mojave Desert. It was definitely scolding him for coming to this place. He'd introduce it to a snack of jackrabbit later. That would keep it happy.

"Damn, you are hot." Selene's voice came from the doorway. How had he not heard her? She blushed. "I mean..."

"I know what you meant. I spend a lot of my time in the mountains in Montana. I'm more acclimatized to snow." He watched her while she placed the food on the table.

"Come on and sit down before the ice cream melts. You look like a cookies n' cream guy. I hope you like it. I'll turn up the AC."

"I can do it."

Surprised, she dodged out of his way when they both reached for the air-conditioning remote control. It was such a quick movement; almost cat-like.

"Please sit. I've already got it."

He took a seat at the table and downed the glass of ice-water in one mouthful. Its cold liquid reduced his body temperature. Selene pressed a button on the remote control, and another icy blast hitting him. He purred as he finally felt relaxed with the cool air washing over him. Thankfully, it was quiet enough that the young human female would not hear him.

"Your mom called when I was downstairs. She shouldn't be long. There was an accident just as she came on the route one-ninety by Death Valley Junction. That's less than half an hour away."

"Great." He needed to have a few words with his mother.

"When was the last time you saw her?" Selene took a seat at the table with him with a small salad she'd brought for herself. No wonder she was tiny if that was all she was eating. The ice cream was good, but he couldn't wait for his mother to cook him a steak or three or, hell, he was on holiday--make that four. Who was he kidding? He wanted the whole cow laid out on his plate. His inner leopard approved of that idea with a smacking lip of its lips.

"It must have been a year now. I don't get here as often as I would like."

"She said your job keeps you busy. park ranger, isn't it?"

"My mom seems to talk about me a lot." He chuckled.

"She's really proud of you." She shrugged. "I think I've pretty much seen all your baby, kindergarten, and graduation pictures, as well as all the school reports. I love the mullet you had going on in high school." It was her turn to laugh.

"Puberty hit me hard."

"You've still got a bit of a mane to you."

"This is nothing in comparison to my friend." He ran his fingers through his hair. He kept long because it did its own thing most of the time. "He has the full fluffy thing happening, no sooner does he style it, does it go poof into a mess again."

"Poor guy."

"What about you?"

"My hair? It does as it's told." She tucked a strand of chestnut hair behind her ear.

He raised an eyebrow at her.

"Oh, you meant who am I?"

"I did. I feel at a disadvantage. You seem to know a great deal about me."

He finished his cookies n' cream, placed the spoon back in the bowl, and popped an ice cube into his mouth to suck.

"There isn't much to know. My name is Selene Harper. I've been working for your mother for six months now-- ever since I arrived in Death Valley. She's given me a room in the apartment with her. It means I can look after the place when she needs to go out."

"How old are you?"

"Twenty-one."

Throughout their entire conversation she'd been keeping eye contact with him, but now she looked down at the salad. Was that a lie? He took a deep inhalation and felt a shift in her scent. She was nervous again. There was something this human was not telling him. He would play along, for now, but when his mother returned he would be demanding answers. Who was this woman living with his mother? Was she safe with her?

"Where did you live before?" Brayden asked.

Selene put her fork down on her plate.

"Look at me stuffing my face and all I've given you is ice cream. I'll tell you what, I'll go and get a burger for you. I'm sure the chief knows how you like it." Was she deliberately avoiding his question?

"There's no need."

"No, no I insist. My lunch break is over anyway. I'll send someone up with it when it's done." She hurried out, leaving him alone with his thoughts.

His mother had emailed him a few months back asking if he could visit her when he could get away. Brayden was the pack's lead enforcer, basically the assassin for the Glacial Blood Pack. A pack, well a family really, brought together by choice, not blood. He was damned good at his job. Recently he'd been kept very busy enough so this was the first chance he'd had to get away.

He'd bet money that whatever his mother wanted to speak to him about, it was related to the waitress. Brayden wasn't going to sit around in his mother's apartment, he was going to go down to the café and observe. His instincts were telling him something was not right here, and he'd learned at a very young age to trust them.

Brayden had just sat in the café with his burger when his mother arrived. He gave her a great big hug, and a contented thrum left his throat. He heard her own hum of pleasure at having her son close.

"I'm sure you've gotten even taller." His mother exclaimed and took a seat opposite to him.

"Compared to Kas, I'm like an ant."

"He always was freakishly big. Your father always said it was the seal blubber. I remember the day I roasted some for him with my grandma's secret spice mix. I don't think I've ever seen a grown man drool so much with anticipation."

"Which reminds me... he wants me to bring another packet of the mix back with me. He's got a hunting trip planned."

"Please tell me he is not going to eat it raw again." Jane raised a questioning eyebrow.

"He likes it that way." Brayden huffed.

"Philistine." His mother rolled her eyes in disgust.

Their conversation quieted when Selene brought his mother a coffee. "Thanks, Sel. How have things been?"

"No problems at all." Selene said. Brayden sat back and started on his burger while the ladies spoke. A perfect medium rare, just as he liked it.

"I see Stuart is in." His mom nodded her head towards a table full of jocks. Their team jackets were thick, despite the high temperature.

"Yes, he wants me to go out with him tonight." Selene stood with her shaking hands clasped in front of her.

"Hi, Mrs. Dillon." One of the men called out. His hair was slicked with gel into a fashionable style and he had a smug smile on his face.

"Hi, Stuart." His mom shouted back before reverting her attention again to Selene. "I thought we might have a nice meal with Brayden?"

"I turned him down last week. I can't really say no again."

"You don't have to go out with him."

"He is good to me." Selene stated quietly.

Brayden could tell by the sudden look of disgust on his mother's face that she didn't believe that.

"And besides, you and your son probably have a lot to catch up on."

"We will do dinner tomorrow. Don't make any plans, please." There was a hint of desperation in his mother's plea.

"You have my word." Selene turned her attention to another patron who had arrived.

"What is going on, Mom?" Brayden asked.

"We'll talk tomorrow, please. Here isn't the place."

"You are worried. We'll talk now."

Someone from the table, at which Stuart sat, loudly called over to Selene. She timidly went over to them.

"Can we get another round of sodas, please? We better get them to go. Don't want to be late for practice. Why don't you see if you can get off and come and join us?" The loud-mouthed idiot, Stuart, grabbed Selene's hand and ran his other hand up her naked leg. Instead of looking like she enjoyed it, the panic-stricken girl looked like she would be sick. A growl formed in Brayden's throat and his fingernails started to shift to claws.

"Brayden, no. She knows what she is doing." His mother placed her hand over his, hiding the sharpened talons. All he could do was watch and keep the reverberations in his throat as quiet as possible. It was his natural state; he couldn't help it. Selene nodded toward where he and his mother sat.

"I wish I could, but Miss Jane needs me." Selene removed Stuart's hand from her leg and kissed it. "But I'll be there when you finish practice, and you can show me that lookout point you wanted to. How about that?"

All Brayden could think about was how could she be all sweetness and light, when it was evident to anyone with half a brain that this man made her skin crawl?

"I suppose that'll do. Make sure you wear a short skirt and show me some skin. That gothic stuff you wear is awful. I never get to see anything with those long skirts."

"I think after a day here it will be a little dirty, but I will see what I can find." With that, Selene disappeared into the back and Brayden could relax. He sheathed his claws again.

"Talk, Mom." After the display he'd just witnessed he wasn't in the mood for arguments.

"I can't here." His mother was panicked.

"Well then let's go upstairs."

"I need to check on Selene."

"Mom. What is going on?" He reached out to grab her hand but she was too quick and got to her feet. He could see tears forming in her eyes.

"Later Brayden. Please, I need you to trust me."

"You know I do, but I can't help if I don't know what is going on." He was on his feet and round to her side of the table pulling her into his arms.

"I will tell you later, but for now, I need you to do one thing for me." She looked up at him. His mother was upset. It ruffled his leopard's fur that she was not telling him how to help.

"What?"

"Tonight, when Selene goes on her date. I need you to follow her," she asked.

"Follow her? If she wants to date that dickhead, why do I need to follow her?"

"You just do. Damn, why are you Dillon males so stubborn and need to know everything? Please, can you do what

I ask for once?" This final plea was frantic.

"Ok. I'll follow her," he replied.

"Thank you. Let whatever happens, happen, but he mustn't touch her."

"Touch her? They are going to a lookout point. I'm pretty confident he plans on doing a lot more than just giving her a kiss."

"He mustn't touch her Brayden, please." His mother was serious; she was worried for this girl.

He held his hands up in surrender. "Alright. He won't."

CHAPTER TWO

She put her head in the toilet bowl and vomited the contents of her lunch directly down the porcelain. Why couldn't she just be normal? Why did she have to be a freak? Standing back up, she flushed the toilet and brushed her teeth. It had been so disgusting. Shuddering in revulsion she wondered how could anyone want that from a woman? Stuart thought of her only as a toy to do his bidding. A knock came to the door. She flicked the lock open, knowing full well who it was.

"Why do you do this to yourself?" Jane, the woman who had become like a mother to her, picked up a towel and wrapped it around her before embracing her.

"I just want to be a typical girl my age." She plopped down on the now closed toilet seat.

"And how old is that?" Jane questioned.

"I don't know." Was the only reply she could give.

"Exactly. Selene, honey, you can never be normal because you're special."

"I don't want to be special." She could feel herself pouting.

"It happened again, didn't it?"

"It happens all the time now. Every day. Whenever anyone touches me, I hear their thoughts." She was still shaking with the feeling of Stuart's filthy mind.

"What was he thinking?"

"Stuart was imagining me naked and riding him. He was using all these dirty words as he got off and covered me in... well you know."

"You cannot go out with him tonight." Jane was pleading with her.

She pushed away from her towards the door. "I have to."

"You don't have to do anything you don't want to."

"I need friends. I have them because Stuart likes the look of me." She snapped back,

"Stuart Henderson likes the look of anything with breasts. He learned from his rich daddy at a very young age how to get what he wants. He's manipulating you." Jane's tone was furious.

"Well, at least I'm doing something right." She stomped into the lounge. Despite the lecture, she was going to do this. "I need to get back downstairs. It's busy with the heat. The kitchen won't cope on their own. "

"I asked Brayden to help out until I could get down there." Jane had followed her.

"He's not stupid. He guessed I'm a freak right away." She could see it in his eyes. "Probably thinking about how he can get the strange girl away from his mother. You know he asked me about myself. Where I came from before living here."

"We made up a story for that." Jane replied.

"And I'm sick of lying."

"Do you remember anything?"

"You know I don't. I'm sorry Jane. I can't talk about this anymore. I'm going back to work and then out on that date."

This time, her surrogate mother didn't stop her, but she kept a watchful eye on her all afternoon. Every time she turned around Jane had her eyes on her. As she dressed for the evening, her mother hovered outside the door. She felt like a child. A prisoner with eyes constantly on her, observing her every move in case she broke. What Jane was doing was to protect her, but how could Selene ever be normal when she shied away from anything that upset her? When it was time to leave for the date, Jane again reiterated that she didn't need to go out. Selene just said her goodbyes and hoped Jane had a good evening with her son.

Her son. Selene couldn't believe that Brayden was here. Jane had emailed to him a few months ago asking him to come. That had been when Selene had first started hearing the thoughts in her head when she touched people. Jane had assured her he could help. Why? What qualifications could a park ranger have that could help her? She would humor Jane if it meant she could find out who she was, and more importantly, what she was. All she knew at the moment was that six months ago she'd woken up in the Death Valley Desert severely dehydrated. If Jane hadn't found her and taken her in, then she would probably be dead. Before that...nothing.

Selene approached Stuart and his teammates standing around his truck. They had a little gang together and called themselves the Rebels of Death. The same name as the football team they played for and of course where they lived. With their wealthy parents, they didn't need to work. Stuart put his arm around her shoulder when she stood next to him.

"I thought I told you to show a bit of flesh tonight?" He frowned.

She looked down at her black maxi dress she was wearing with a long-sleeved silk cardigan in light blue.

"I...er...got cold."

"If you want to be my girlfriend Sel, you've got to look good. I need all my team to be jealous that I'm dating the prettiest girl out there." He spoke with a cocky edge to his voice. He was the son of the town's richest resident. His father thought he owned Furnace Creek.

"I'll try harder next time." She gave him a polite smile while trying not to throw up...again.

"Make sure you do. Come on, get in the truck. We'll go for a ride." Most of the other players dispersed to whatever they would be getting up to that evening. Stuart opened the door of his truck for her. "Joe and Callie are coming up to the point when she can get away from her mother. She flipped out when she found Callie's condoms earlier. The girl's eighteen, for fuck's sake. She can put out if she wants to."

"Yeah, her mother should stay out of it. She and Joe love

each other." She tried to put enthusiasm into her reply, but she wondered if Callie's mother just didn't want her daughter trapped in Death Valley with a loser like Joe. Selene knew she was an idiot for getting involved with these guys. They would never amount to anything more than football wannabes, but she wanted to make friends her own age. Well, what she thought was her own age.

Stuart helped her into the truck, and they made the short drive with rock music blaring on his stereo. The moon shone brightly in the clear night sky. When they arrived, Stuart left her to get out of the truck herself while he lit up a cigarette. She relaxed against the hood with her feet dangling down to observe the view.

"You were right." She commented with amazed breathlessness. "It's lovely up here. You can really see the variations in the rock formations. We could almost be on a different planet."

"If you want to play aliens and invading astronauts I'm up for that." He winked at her.

"You can be such a dork sometimes."

"A cute dork, though, you must admit." He snuggled in a little closer, and she tried to keep her breathing calm, but the nerves were threatening to engulf her. "Look, Sel I know you're scared." He actually sounded as though he was trying to reassure her. "I guessed the first time I met you that you were a virgin. I'm not going to lie. I've got a big dick. It's going to hurt when we first have sex, but I promise I'll make you feel good. I've got to keep my reputation intact after all. Can't be known for disappointing my girlfriend, now can I?"

"Stuart, I just don't think I'm ready for sex, yet. Please. I'm sorry."

"I can't say I'm happy about that. I want you, but we can do other stuff." He grabbed her arm, over the silk cardigan, and directed her covered hand over the hard bulge in his jeans. "You can't leave me like this another night, babe. Every time I'm near you I have to go home and jerk off.

You've got to at least suck me off this time."

Suck him off. That would mean her lips would be touching his cock. Skin on skin. She'd put a thick layer of lip balm on her lips earlier, as they were dry. Maybe that would protect her.

"Come on babe. Just touch it." She looked down at his crotch while she was reflecting. He'd removed himself from his jeans. He was big like he'd said, but given she'd never seen a penis before, other than in pictures, she didn't really have much to compare it to. He grabbed her hand again and wrapped it around his dick. Thankfully her long sleeves prevented her from being skin on skin. He started to move her hand up and down his length. Her eyes were wide, taking in the act. She was touching someone and judging by the fact his eyes were shut, and he had a smile on his face, he was enjoying it. She could be normal.

"Oh, fuck babe that is good, but this shirt needs to go." Before she could protest, he had ripped the silk from her shoulders and thrown it on the dusty floor. He wrapped his fingers around her hand and helped her stroke his length again.

'Goddam dirty whore.'

The words popped into her head. Stuart's thoughts.

'Come on bitch, take some initiative and suck me.'

He pulled her towards him like a rag doll; held the back of her head and thrust it into his groin. He was leaning against the truck. She was millimetres away from a purple-headed giant looking at her, its thick veins flexing.

"Suck me, Selene."

'Stick my fucking cock in your goddamn mouth and suck me dry or I going to pin you down and fucking take that dirty little whore's mouth. You act all innocent, but I know you want it. Nobody can resist me.'

She just wanted to be normal so lowered her warm and wet mouth around his penis. The thoughts in her head magnified, pounding into her shaking body.

'That's it. Oh God, yes. I will be fucking your tight little cunt

before the evening is out. You're so weak, like all the other women. Give them a big cock, and you can get whatever you need.'

She couldn't take it anymore. She couldn't do this. Pulling away, she thrust herself from the truck.

"What the fuck!" The words echoed in the still of the desert night.

"I want to go home." She wrapped her arms around her body. "Take me home."

"Get back here and suck my cock."

"Take me home." She shouted in reply.

Stuart pushed away the vehicle, and she was relieved to see he was putting himself back into his jeans.

"You're not going anywhere, babe. I brought you out here to get fucked, and that is precisely what is going to happen."

He pushed her against a rock formation and started to bunch her dress up. Before he got a chance to touch her flesh, she kicked in him the leg.

"Bitch!" He pulled his arm back and went to swing a punch into her face. She shut her eyes tightly. The pain of a beating never arrived though. Instead, it was Stuart who called out in agony. She opened her eyes to see Brayden fling him against the side of the truck.

"I do believe the lady said no." She was pretty sure he growled.

Stuart righted himself from the impact of the car and went towards Brayden with his fists raised. Jane's son dodged the angry jock--the most surreal movement she had ever seen; like it played out in slow motion. Stuart turned and aimed a fist again, but Brayden twisted his arm around his back and rammed him into the truck a second time.

"This is your first and only warning. The lady said no, so get back in your car and return home." Brayden snarled into Stuart's ear.

"What the fuck is your problem? Don't you know who I am?" Stuart was pushing back, trying to use his footballer strength to break free.

"If necessary I will put you back in this car, lock the doors and send it flying over the lookout point." Brayden pulled him back and slammed into him again in a football tackle.

"You and what army?" Stuart angrily replied.

"I don't need an army. Now, are you going to do as I say, or shall we test my idea?"

Brayden let go of Stuart, who headed to the driver's side of his car and got in. Through the open window, he called out.

"This isn't over yet. You'll regret interfering." He slammed the truck into reverse and sped backward before stopping again, close to Selene. "And you, bitch, you just made yourself an outcast in this town. Might as well move on, now." With that, he put the truck in drive and disappeared in a cloud of dust leaving her coughing.

Selene collapsed on the ground shaking, trying to catch her breath. Brayden crouched down to check on her. What was he even doing here?

"Your mother asked you to follow me, didn't she?"

He turned. His bright green eyes focused directly upon her in the moonlight. They seemed bigger than normal.

"She asked me to make sure Stuart didn't touch you. It seems she was right to worry."

"I've been such a fool." She sighed.

"You're young, you want to experience new things, but take a word of advice from me. Do it with someone who isn't a complete jerk."

"I wanted him to help me make friends."

"Friends aren't everything. Sometimes being your own person in solitude is safer and a lot more fulfilling." Selene could still feel the angry heat radiating off of him.

"I get the feeling you like spending time alone," she replied.

"It's my nature."

"Nature?"

"Spending time alone in the mountains." He looked to the ground and picked up a stone and threw it away.

"Oh."

She got to her feet and Brayden stood with her.

"Thank you for helping me. It's difficult to explain. I don't like touching people and what he wanted me to do... it was too much. I'll tell Jane everything and make sure there are no repercussions for her."

She was right in front of him now. The fear she had felt turned to a feeling of safety.

"I'll take you home, we can explain it together." He reached out as if to take her hand but then realized what she had said about touch and dropped his arm back to his side.

"My car is down the road a bit. I couldn't risk being heard. Be careful on the rocks as we go down."

In all her life, she had never willingly reached out to touch someone, but she found herself doing it before she could think. She took his hand, and hers was enveloped in his grip. No thoughts entered her head. Her hand began to tingle. Both their gazes shifted to where they were joined, skin to skin. Her hand was changing, fingers turning into a paw, nails into claws. Fur sprouted through the skin in white and smoky gray flecks. The hair was spreading, her arm changing into a... a cat's leg. She jumped back, breaking the connection, her arm cradled to her chest. Slowly the effects of the touch reversed until she returned to normal.

"Selene," Brayden spoke but his words were lost.

All she could do was stare at her hand. "Wh... what are you?" she stuttered.

"You need to let me take you back to my mother's apartment now." He stepped forward, but she jumped back again.

"Don't touch me." Selene snapped frantically and shrunk away covering her body. She was terrified.

He held his hands out in front of him so she could see them. "I won't. You have my word. Let's go down to the car.

Mom can help me explain."

"She's like you? No, I've touched her. I heard her thoughts. I didn't start changing into...into what was that?"

"Selene, please, the car." He stepped forward again and tried to wrap his arms around her. She was too quick for him though, kicking out before taking off through the desert as fast as she could. She didn't have a clue where she was going. She just knew she needed to get away. The darkness was closing in. The last thing she wanted was to be stranded in the California desert with no water. A noise came from her left and she froze. From the shadows stalked a big cat. It got close enough that she could distinguish it as a snow leopard. Recognition, shook her. It couldn't be. Her hand, that was what she had been changing into.

"Brayden?"

The form in front of her shifted into the naked, toned masculine form of Brayden. "I can't leave you out here alone."

"You changed. The cat?" Her voice was quivering.

"I will explain, but I need you to come with me." He stepped forward and she stepped back straightening her spine.

"Not happening. You tell me here and now. I'm not going anywhere with something that could eat me." She was adamant.

"You'd need more meat on your bones for me to eat you. You're perfectly safe," he flippantly replied.

"Fuck you." she quipped with an annoyed smirk.

In a quick movement, that she hadn't seen coming he held a stick to his mouth and blew. She felt a sharp pain in her neck and raised her hand to it. A dart rested in her neck. Why would someone carry that with them? How had he carried it in Snow leopard form? In his tail? What had she gotten herself involved in?

"You drugged me...."

The last thing she remembered was the ground rapidly heading up to meet her face. It never hit, though. Instead warm, masculine hands wrapped around her.

CHAPTER THREE

Selene was cold, so very cold. That was the first thing that hit her. The second was the massive headache from whatever it was Brayden had drugged her with. She still had her eyes shut. She didn't appear to be in pain, other than her head. At least he hadn't started eating her yet. Had he dragged her back to his cave? Did snow leopards live in caves? Or maybe she was dead? That could be why she was so cold.

"You have water and painkillers beside the bed that will help with your headache. I'll get you another blanket out of the cupboard. You will acclimatize to the colder weather soon." She froze at the deep voice close to her and opened one eye. A muscular man sat in the sparsely decorated room looking at her from an antique rocking chair. If it was possible, he looked even bigger than Brayden. From the look of him, he would be in his late thirties.

"Where am I?" she asked.

"Montana." His voice was deep and commanding. His dark eyes were almost jet black in color. He had peppering of white flecks in his hair.

"How?"

"Private jet."

"Brayden?" She knew instantly who had brought her here. Where was he?

"He is downstairs resting. I'm afraid you gave him quite a fright."

"I gave him a fright? Are you joking? Are you the same as him?" She winced at the lack of strength in her voice.

The man laughed, his gruff voice echoing in the room.

"If you mean am I a snow leopard, then I take that as a bit of an insult. May I approach you?" Selene shrunk back at that question.

"Do I have a choice?"

"I'd like to think so. I'm not going to force you into anything you don't want." There was genuine honesty in his words.

"Then put me on whatever private jet brought me here and let me go back to California."

Understanding she had already been forced into coming to Montana without her consent, "Ahh good point. However, I'm afraid, you have must stay here for the time being."

"So what you're saying is, as long as I do what you say I have some freedom of choice." That was a scary thought. She was a captive here.

"Correct."

"Why are you speaking to me and not Brayden?"

"I'm the leader here."

"Leader?" she asked.

"Of the Glacial Blood Pack. Yes, I am. My name is Kaskae but people call me Kas. My name is Inuit for leader. My family named our children with their aspirations for them. Now, I believe I asked if I could approach you. The common courtesy is an answer."

"And as I asked, do I have a choice?"

"You do have quite the attitude on you."

"I don't normally, but being drugged and taken from my home tends to leave me in a bad mood." He ignored her comment and stood beside the bed she was in.

"I'm intrigued as to what Brayden told me happened between you. Would you hold your hand out for me?"

"I'm not going to touch you."

"It would give us both the answers we seek."

"And you can go fuck yourself."

"Miss Harper. I'm sure, at the moment, you must be very scared, so I will forgive your outbursts. I would ask you to assist with our questions. It will be beneficial to you."

She didn't reply, just held her hand out with a roll of her eyes.

"Thank you." He held his hand out to touch her. The new yet familiar tingling started and her hand began to change. This time, the pads turned into five small circles, not the four of cats. Her fingernails turned into sharp black claws that did not retract, and the fur that grew was hollow and thick. Kas was a polar bear. Didn't they have black skin? She pulled her hand away. Her mouth dried.

"Amazing." Kas stood there staring at his own hand.

Selene let out a loud shriek.

****

Brayden shuddered at the scream from above. He wanted to go to her, but he'd been told to stay away for now. He'd been sitting in a lounge chair staring out the window for an hour now. He loved this house. It was the only home he'd ever lived in. It was late 1800's in design, a brick built Victorian mansion that was made to last. It had curved Gothic style windows with the wooden frames painted royal blue. A lot of the furniture matched the era with soft chaise and solid wood cabinets. His favorite was an antique grandfather clock in the hallway. It didn't always chime the correct hour but at least it still told the time. The chair he was sitting in was marked as his own. His inner leopard had enjoyed scratching a 'B' on the wooden leg. During meetings it allowed him to sit on the periphery of the discussion, only giving input when vital. He was a snow leopard. They spent most of their time alone. Even when a male had impregnated the females in the wilds, he often disappeared to find another. The female would raise her cubs alone and then they would leave to follow the same path. They didn't stay with anyone for very long. To be surrounded by so many people often lead Brayden to feel claustrophobic, and that is when he would take to his chair and stare at the mountains.

"Hey Bray, couldn't stand the heat?" Scott, a male lion

shifter, entered the room and threw himself down on the sofa with a leg of lamb in his mouth.

"You get blood on the couch and Kas will have you cleaning it with your tongue." Brayden rolled his eyes.

"Right now I think he's more intrigued with what the cat dragged home." Scott reply was quick witted.

"You know I'm trained well enough to shove that lamb bone where the sun doesn't shine, don't you?" He shut his eyes and groaned.

"You wouldn't do that to me. Who would help you on all your scavenger hunts up the mountain?" The lion was overly confident with that answer.

"Emma, like she normally does, while you sit there and lick your arse." Scott was a typical male lion, ferocious when needed, but lazy as hell when not. He also ate like nobody Brayden had ever seen. Scott was very rarely without something in his mouth. Brayden wasn't only talking about food. Scott had a harem of women he often visited to get satisfaction for his libido. Again, typical male lion behaviour. Scott had joined the pack a few years ago. Male lions were kicked out of their packs when they reached maturity. He suspected because they were good for nothing and the females did not want to look after them. The Glacial Blood Pack had invited him back to dinner once and he'd never left.

"My ass tastes a lot better than those vegetable things that you eat."

"Vegetables are good for you."

"Strange cat. Probably the reason that your coat isn't as glossy as mine."

"My coat is designed for warmth. Yours is for showing off and attracting all the nubile females to do your bidding." He rolled his eyes again when the lion looked smug.

"Seriously man, what is going on with this chick? You skulk home in the middle of the night with a woman over your shoulder and wake us all up. I know that Kas wants you to mate and everything but bringing her home, drugged, after one day away?"

"She isn't my mate. In fact, I suspect at this very moment she'd love to see me dead." He still couldn't believe that he'd drugged Selene. It was part of the kit they carried with them in case something like that was needed. He'd felt so guilty using it on her though. And ashamed; it was hardly a kickarse gun but then they were incredibly difficult to keep curled up in your tail. She was so confused and scared, he had shot her like prey.

"But Kas told me you touched her, and she started changing?" Scott shifted in the chair, leaning forward with the lamb bone in his mouth.

"Yes," he replied, remorse evident in his answer.

"What is she?"

"I think that is what Kas is trying to find out."

"You know you did the right thing bringing her here."

"Really?" Brayden wasn't so sure. She was terrified. She'd thought he was going to eat her. He disappeared into his thoughts. It had made him so angry the way Stuart had touched her, forcing her to wrap those perfect lips around his cock. Wait, had he actually thought her lips were perfect? Well they were. She was a stunning girl and going through so much. She had bravery, a trait that would serve him well as a mate. She'd look lovely with her lips around his cock. What a beautiful daydream. Scott crunching on the bone brought him back to the here and now. Ok, he needed to stop thinking like this. She hated him, wanted him dead.

"Brayden, you did the right thing in bringing Miss Harper here." Kas entered the room and took a seat in his favorite chair. "That girl is unique."

"You touched her."

"I did."

A pang of anger rumbled within him. She must be so scared, and here was Kas forcing her to be a performing monkey. "She changed into a polar bear is that why she screamed?" Brayden concluded.

"I'm afraid it scared her a little. To me it was a beautiful thing."

"You only think that because she became a mirror of you."

"She changed into a polar bear, but it was not my mirror. She is much smaller. I would say she would have been a cub if she'd fully changed."

"You didn't make her turn all the way?"

"We don't know the possible effects. Prudence says we should experiment, or we risk damage to the subject. That is why I've sent for Jessica."

"She is not an experiment."

"Kas won't do anything to her and neither will you." His mother slammed in through the door. "She is coming home with me." The expression on her face was deadlier than any predator that he had ever faced.

"Mrs. Dillon." Scott scrambled towards the door. "Nice to see you again but I think I hear a female lion in need." He couldn't get out of the room quick enough. Brayden wished he could follow. He'd face down anything but his mother at this precise moment.

"Jane, you know we cannot allow that to happen. She is of vital importance to us and also a possible risk."

"I don't care what you do or do not allow Kaskae. I'm taking Selene with me. She's an innocent in all this. I called Brayden for help in discovering where she comes from, not to have her used as a pawn in your games. Now, where is she?"

"I see now why your father often disobeyed my rules, Brayden." Kas rested one of his long legs on top of the other.

"Leave my father out of this."

"I was merely making an observation on the persistence of your mother."

"Don't." He sprang to his feet. His temper was wearing thin now. He'd gone on vacation to spend time with his mother and all hell had broken loose. He hadn't slept in twenty-four hours. The burger he'd had in the cafe had been his last meal. He'd never even gotten his steak! His leopard growled within him at the thought. He was so hungry.

Kas got to his own feet and used his superior height to try to intimidate Brayden. It never worked. Brayden was silent and deadly. In a flash, he punched Kas and was ready to go again. His mother shouted at him to stop.

Jane jumped in front of them. "This won't help anything. What is done is done. Now we need to concentrate on Selene."

"I need to know more about her. If she is dangerous..." Kas said.

"Not happening." Brayden puffed up again. Nobody would hurt Selene.

"Brayden. Take a seat. I need to tell you both what I know."

He gave one more growl in Kas' direction before slumping back into his chair. Kas resumed his seat and motioned for his mother to do the same. She took a chair in between them.

"I first met her about six months ago. I was driving through Death Valley on my way back from a meeting in the heart of it. It was late. There was a flash, and down the road, I saw something weaving along the road. It was Selene. She was naked and pale and barely able to stand. I managed to talk her into the car with me. I brought her back to the apartment and gave her food and drink. I should have taken her to the hospital, but she refused to go. When I asked her how she got there, she couldn't remember. She said that she just woke up from what felt like a very long sleep."

"She has no idea where she is from?" Kas sat back in his chair as he replied. His hand was placed at his chin in thought. It was a stance that Brayden knew meant the polar bear was deadly serious in his questioning.

"As far as she is concerned, her life only started the

moment she woke in the heat of the night in Death Valley."

"What about the thoughts?" Kas asked.

"That started about three months after she arrived. One day, she dropped some plates. She'd been shaky and not feeling well all day. I touched her arm while she was looking down at the mess. I thought that she needed to sleep. She told me she would lie down when she'd tidied up. I hadn't said anything, but I was still touching her arm. Ever since it's been getting stronger and stronger. It wasn't all the time at first, but now it is. She feels so much anguish when anyone comes near her because she knows that she will hear whatever is in their head if she so much as brushes against their skin."

"Was Brayden the first shifter she touched?"

"We don't get to many shifters in the café. I'm sure all my belongings smell like Heath's. It wouldn't surprise if Brayden's scent is everywhere too so they probably avoid it. I don't have a radar for them like you do so I'm not sure that I would know."

"When I was there the first time, I caught the scent of coyotes. I made sure to mark all-round the café. I top it up when I go back each time. I'm don't like having those rabid canines near my mother."

"That was wise. I will get Jessica to look into a more permanent solution for protection." Kas nodded.

"Who is Jessica?"

Brayden rarely talked about the pack with his mother. She knew most of the members from when she was with his father. When she left, though, he wanted her to have her freedom. "Jessica is a witch."

"She will discover what Selene is. Brayden, Jane, I must warn you both now, though--if she is a danger to the pack, then you know the decision I have to make."

His mom looked over at him, and he could see the tears forming in her eyes. If Kas tried to hurt Selene, then Brayden would do everything in his power to stop him.

CHAPTER FOUR

Selene rattled the bars on the window, but they would not give.

"Damn it! Break. Please." She had been doing the same thing for more than half an hour. If only she could get the bars that kept her prisoner to move! She could see a gable and trellis outside. She could climb down to the ground and make a run for it. If she stayed here for much longer, she was sure the freaky bear with the scowl would enjoy her as an appetizer.

A commotion outside the window drew her attention. She was going to shout for help but found herself watching as a couple fought, with a crowd of others observing. By all rights the male should flatten the female with one punch-- he must have been at least twice her size--but she held her own. She was weaving and spinning against his strong attack and then forming her own in her endeavour to weaken him.

She caught him on the side of the face and he lurched backward. The crowd cheered their delight but booed when the male started to shift. His body began to cover in golden fur, his legs transformed into those of a strong feline with claws. His hair, which had been untamed anyway, grew darker and fuller until it resembled a mane. The man had turned, before her very eyes, into a lion. He shook off his clothes and pounced at the female. He was going to kill her.

Before the lion could attack, the female had shifted into a beautiful lioness, her sleek body rippling with muscles of strength. They fought on until she was trapped under the male. The man licked her face, and she shifted back to human.

"Yuck, Scott. If you are going to insist on working your

snacks off by playing, then at least brush your teeth first. Your breath stinks."

"But how would I be able to impress you with my ability to find food then?" The lion had shifted back to human form as well. Their naked bodies pressed against each other, the man's tight backside fully on display. Selene felt a warmth between her thighs and rubbed them together.

"I can ask Kas if I can take you down to watch them if you want." The voice made her jump. She spun around and found Brayden standing before her with a tray of food. The door was open. Without thinking too much, she ran. The food clattered to the floor.

"Selene." He reached out and grabbed her bare arm. Her breath hitched as the tingling started and the fur began to grow. She stared at it spreading up her arm, further than it did before, over her chest and down towards her stomach. She could feel bones breaking and reforming within her, yet there was no pain. Brayden pulled his hand away and held his arms up. The fur vanished as quickly as it had appeared and her insides returned to normal. She thought that hearing what people were thinking was bad, but this? She couldn't understand it. What was she? Was she even human? Why was this happening to her? How could she stop it?

Too many questions, not enough answers. She broke.

***

He hadn't meant to touch her again.

She'd almost become a full snow leopard. He hadn't been able to do anything but stare. She was beautiful.

He pulled a sheet from the bed and wrapped it around her before carrying her to the bed and positioning her on his lap so that he could comfort her while she cried. Every tear was like a dagger through his heart. She had his protection. He would do everything that he could so that she'd never have to cry like this again.

What the hell was happening to him? This was not the man he was. He was changing. She was changing him.

***

Selene wasn't sure how long she'd been crying, but her body ached. Even though she still let out hiccupping sobs, no more tears fell from her eyes. Brayden was still holding her, the warmth of his body like a protective blanket. No part of his skin was touching her, but she knew he was there and that he was worried about her. She should push him away. Scream, shout, run for the door, but her body wouldn't move.

"I'm sorry I brought you here. At the time, I thought it was for the best. It's the rules of my pack, my family if you can understand the similarity. If a human sees our true forms, then we have to bring them to Kas to deal with. It's the only way to protect who, what, we are. I didn't realize that he'd make you change for him. I won't let him do it again."

"This is your family? What about Jane?"

"Jane is my biological mother. She was sixteen when she met my father and had me. He was a pure snow leopard shifter. His family can be traced back to the great leopard kings of Hermes National Park in India. I don't know too much about the details of how they met, but I know she found out quite quickly that he was a snow leopard. I guess he told her when she became pregnant. My mother was, and still is the only human who has been accepted into the pack, though we are not elitist like some packs out there. We accept those that need a family."

"There are more?"

"I'm afraid to tell you that there are all sorts of shifters in the world, not just the ones you have seen here. Some are pure breeds, others are hybrid. Some live alone, some in packs."

"I never knew any of this existed. Then again, it's not as

if I know very much." She sighed. "What about the others?"

Kas, and those you saw downstairs fighting, they are what I call my Glacial Blood family. We are not the same blood, but that doesn't mean we are not family. We exist to protect each other and live together. I guess 'glacial blood' is a play on words."

"Good. For a minute, I thought you were going to tell me you had vampires here as well."

"No vampires here. There are vampire bat shifters but not in our pack. "I'm a snow leopard, Kas is a polar bear, we have two lions, Scott and Emma, Katia is a tiger-lioness hybrid, a wolf called Tyler and a brown bear called Zain. That is the pack that live here. We have additional people around the world though but I prefer to just interact with a few people. Plus, we have Jessica, she is a witch."

"No vampires but witches. Got it." If her head wasn't going to explode before, it was now.

"How did you all meet?"

"Kas' family owns the land we are on."

"I thought it was a national park." She raised a taunting eyebrow.

"That is what we allow the humans to think." Brayden smirked.

"Silly me."

"He met my father shortly after he'd taken over as the leader. They were young and became good friends. When my dad died, I was given a place for life in the pack. Zain arrived when I was fifteen. He was seventeen and had been traveling for at least a year. We think he was running away from something, but he's very quiet and doesn't talk about his past. Jessica and Kas were friends from youth. When she split from her lover, she became a permanent member here. Katia and Tyler grew up here. Their parents were here for several years. They are still on the land but not in the main day-to-day part of the pack anymore. They are enjoying a well-earned retirement."

"You mentioned an Emma?"

"Emma is like a little sister to me. She was abandoned by her family as a baby. We have a Council that governs all shifters, that's what we call ourselves. It's all very secret. Anyway, the Council asked Kas to take Emma in. We had a few females around then that were able to nurse her. Kas will never turn away a stray."

She pulled away from him and sat up so that she could look directly into his jade eyes. He still held her hand through the sheet.

"This is a lot to take in, isn't it?" Brayden asked.

"Almost as much as it probably is for you to see me change when you touch me." she smiled.

"Yes, that was a bit of a shock. I was bracing myself not to think about being a snow leopard. I really didn't expect you to grow fur instead."

"What is going to happen to me?"

"Kas is going to help you discover who and what you are. Mom is downstairs. She wasn't impressed that I took you. I'm just glad I'm too big to go over her knee. Though I don't think I'm getting any steak from her in the foreseeable future."

Food. She pulled her hand away. "What do you eat?"

"Are you asking me if we eat humans?"

"Yes." Now wasn't the time to beat around the bush, Selene thought.

"No, we don't eat humans. Yes, we have killed people before when they have threatened the safety of the pack. We have been respectful and given them a proper burial on consecrated ground based on their religion. As for what we eat, well you've already seen me eat ice cream and a burger. I even ate the lettuce you put in it. Snow leopards are rare in the cat world in that we eat vegetation with our meat. We go to the shops like anyone else and buy meat, we just generally prefer it rare. If we are up in the mountains or on a hunt, then we eat wild animals. Kas loves seals, he requires a lot of blubber in his diet. Zain is typically found in a lake after fish or with his hand in a bee hive after the honey.

"Doesn't that hurt?"

"You would think so, but apparently not. They can't penetrate his long fur. It's actually quite funny to watch. He shoves his hand in and grabs the comb. Then makes a dash for it, shaking them all off him like water droplets. It's normally the other guys and I who get stung."

"You seem very close, despite obvious differences in your natures."

"We are. Like I said, they are my family--brothers and sisters."

"It's nice. You have the playful nature. I saw that with the two lions fighting. It looked savage, but every movement was orchestrated not to hurt."

"We are just like a litter of clubs playing, really."

"That's a good analogy."

Brayden wrapped his hands within the sheet and took both of hers in his.

"Selene, I know I scared you the other night. What I did with the dart, bringing you here. I'm sorry. I panicked."

"Yes, you did, but then, I'm not exactly normal."

"You want to find out where you come from. That is why my mom called me, isn't it?"

"Yes."

"Here and now, you have my word. Together we will find out." Tears started to form in Selene's eyes, it had been such a stressful few hours. In fact, it had been a nightmarish six months. She had no idea where she'd come from or even what she was doing here. But in this moment, with Brayden's ardent stare telling her she could trust him, she was finally feeling relaxed--that she wasn't something bad and evil, or someone's dinner. Maybe she had a purpose, and together they would find out what.

"Thank you." They both moved closer, their lips inches apart. Was this to be a kiss? Was this to be a chance at hope?

A knock at the door broke the trance. Brayden pulled away and jumped off the bed. The door opened and the woman she'd seen shift into a lioness earlier entered.

"Sorry to interrupt. Kas wants us all in the lounge. Miss Harper, as well. Jessica is here."

CHAPTER FIVE

Brayden sat on his chair, his strong hand stroking the rough stubble on his jaw. Selene stood in the middle of the room surrounded by the pack. His mother sat beside him and Kas reclined in his usual chair.

"Zain, you go first." Kas' commanding voice bellowed out his instructions.

"Why do we have to do this? Surely we know she changes." The big bear folded his arms across his chest.

"We need to just test the strength of Selene's powers. Ensure that it is all animals she shifts with and not just certain ones," Jessica told Zain.

"Ok, I'll do it, but if she changes and goes after my honey, then I won't be a happy bear."

Brayden tried not to laugh. Zain was always very protective of his honey. He had pots of the stuff in a cupboard in his room and kept it locked and the key on him at all times.

"Zain." This time it was Selene's turn to provide reassurance. "I promise you, I will not touch your honey. It is safe. I'm not a big fan of it anyway."

"You don't like honey?" Zain's face looked incredulous. "She doesn't like honey." Zain turned to Brayden. "Is that why she is so small?"

"She might be small, but she packs a punch. I've still got bruises to prove it, and there is a jock in Death Valley who is probably still singing falsetto after she hit him in the balls."

Zain whipped his head back to Selene, "New rule, she can have all the honey that she wants, but she has to leave my testicles alone."

Kas groaned and put his head in his hands.

Selene said, "I promise you, Zain, your testicles are safe."

I think you better touch me so we can see if I change, or Kas might go after your honey." Zain growled in Kas' direction. The polar bear responded in kind. Selene took matters into her own hands and touched Zain's flesh. Her hand started to shift into a bear's paw.

"Enough," Kas called out, and Brayden saw Zain jump back. Selene returned to her natural state. "Tyler, your turn."

Brayden watched as Tyler stepped forward and touched Selene. She again started to shift—into a wolf. Emma and Scott followed, while Selene stayed true to her sex and became a lioness.

Next up was Katia, the lion-tiger hybrid.

"You're a tiger and lion, aren't you?" Selene queried.

"Yes, my mother is a white tiger and my father a lion."

"A hybrid, like Brayden is."

"With Brayden, I change to a snow leopard, what will I change to with Katia?" Selene turned to ask Jessica.

"I'm not sure. It could be both, or it could be the more dominant. With Brayden, his leopard side is the strongest because humans are weak." She looked at Jane, "No offense, Mrs. Dillon."

"None taken." Thankfully, his mother smiled.

"The only way we will know is if you touch her."

"Okay." Selene stepped forward. Brayden leaned forward in his seat, as intrigued as everyone else by what she would change into. Her body began to transform. Golden fur. No stripes. Katia's touch turned Selene into a lioness.

"Yes, lions rule." Scott jumped up and pumped his fists into the air.

"It would indeed appear that my father's genes are the stronger of my two. I secretly hoped you would be at least a little bit tiger."

"I'm sorry. If I could explain it, I would try to make me more tiger."

Katia laughed, and Selene joined in. It was the first time since they'd had lunch together that Brayden had heard her laugh. It lit up the room.

He adjusted his position, his suddenly-tight jeans needing a bit more space.

"When Katia shifts, is she mainly lion?"

"Katia shift." Jessica had caught onto Selene's train of thought. The tigress removed her clothes. This time it was Selene's turn to blush. She'd get used to the nakedness. Especially with Tyler's penchant for removing his clothes whenever possible. Katia shifted into her natural state, a brilliant white lion with jet black stripes.

"Wow, she's beautiful." Katia rubbed against Selene's long skirt in a thank you. She reached down, and when she stroked the tigress black and white stripes appeared on Selene's arm. Katia shifted back to human and hugged Selene tightly.

"Katia, could we please put Miss Harper down? I think you may be scaring her." Kas shook his head.

"Sorry. I'm just so happy that my stronger form as an animal is a tiger. Tigers rock." She stuck her tongue out at Scott, who just rolled his eyes and went back to scratching behind his ear with his foot.

"So, Brayden is stronger as an animal in both his forms?"

"Did you touch him when he shifted?"

She looked at him. Had she? Brayden couldn't really remember.

"I don't think so."

"No, I think I just froze. I was probably too worried about being eaten by my boss' son than to think about stroking the pretty kitty behind the ear."

"I'm not a pretty kitty." He hissed back at her.

"Sorry, a great big manly specimen of leopard-hood." Selene taunted.

"Better." Brayden smugly folded his arms over his chest.

"Do you want to test the theory?" Jessica proposed.

"I'm not entirely sure Selene should be reading his thoughts at the moment." Tyler howled with laughter.

"What, you scared that she might find out I'm planning

on eating you for dinner tonight?" Brayden rasped out a commanding response.

"I'd like to see you try." The wolf puffed up.

"Children." Jane interrupted. "Brayden, shift so we can see. Selene needs to know everything she can about her abilities."

He stood and shifted before shaking out of his clothes.

"I hope you don't expect me to tidy them up." His mother sighed behind him as he padded towards Selene. The young waitress was shaking, and his keen eyesight let him see her take a deep swallow. She'd not been as scared of Katia in tiger/lion form. He could smell the fear coming from her. Why was she so afraid of him?

Slowly she got down onto her knees before him. Her head bowed. He moved around her, being careful not to touch her flesh. The room had gone silent. He was marking her with his scent before them. She was his. He stopped in front of her, his face inches from hers. She lifted her hand, and he growled softly. She hesitated and swallowed again. He mewled and jerked his head to let her know she could touch him. She stroked her hand down his head, and fur and claws started to appear. She let out a long breath, and he purred. He shifted back, and she averted her eyes when he stood naked before her.

"Brayden, please warn your mother before you shift." He looked to his mother who had her hands over her eyes."

"Sorry, Mom."

"So, it would seem that Brayden is strongest as an animal as well. You cannot read any of our thoughts as we are predominately animals." Kas spoke while Brayden grabbed his clothes and dressed.

"It would appear so, but I'm interested to see what happens next." Jessica stepped forward.

"You are human, surely I will just hear your thoughts." Selene returned to her feet and stood directly in front of Jessica.

"I don't know what will happen. If you touch me, it

could blow this room up. Or nothing will happen. Or you will just hear my thoughts."

"Okay, then."

"Do you still need us?" Tyler stood. "I thought maybe we could..."

"Sit Tyler. Proceed, Jessica."

Selene reluctantly held her hand out, and Jessica took it in a firm hold. Brayden held his breath, and a green hue started to travel up Selene's arm. Both women watched as pagan symbols began to appear all over her skin. The transformation happened much more quickly that it did for changing to an animal. In a matter of seconds, Selene had completely transformed. Jessica took her other hand.

"I'd almost forgotten what a witch's natural state looked like."

"Green with weird symbols it seems." Selene didn't look too sure about what was happening to her.

"I want to try something. Do you consent?"

"It doesn't involve trying to blow the room up?"

"No. I want you to do a small spell. You see the chair I was sitting in? I'm going to clear my mind and incant a few words, and I want you to concentrate on the chair rising up off the floor. Normally I would do both. I want to see if while joined we can split the magic."

Selene looked over to Brayden, and he gave her a nod.

"Imagine the chair rising up. Got it?"

Jessica shut her eyes only to open them moments later to reveal clear white orbs where her eyes had been. Selene tried to pull her hands back, but the witch held tight.

"I don't know if I want to do this." Selene was panic-stricken. Brayden had seen Jessica go like this on numerous occasions, but for a first time, on top of everything else, it was probably pushing Selene's boundaries.

Kas looked over to him, willing him to reassure her.

"Selene, you can do this. We are all here for you." Being a team player wasn't really his strength.

"Please."

He got to his feet and went to her. Without touching her skin, he placed his hands on her shoulders.

"I'm here. Look at the chair. Imagine it flying. Like the birds in Death Valley."

"You mean the vultures?"

"Whatever helps."

She looked at the chair, her stare narrowing as she focused on it. He lifted his hands but made no movement to return to his seat. Selene would be able to feel him close.

"Rise." The word tumbled from her lips, and at the same time, Jessica started to chant her spell. "Rise, rise, rise."

Everybody focused on the chair. It started to wobble. Selene's breath hitched. The chair lifted off the ground, into the air, and slammed into the ceiling. People yelled as it smashed into pieces and parts of the ceiling came falling down. Selene pulled her hands away from Jessica and thrust herself into his chest, her hands outstretched behind him, so she didn't touch his flesh.

Jessica returned to the living world.

"Wow. I didn't expect it to work that well. It appears that you not only take on my powers but also amplify them. That could be very useful."

"You know what Selene is?" It suddenly dawned on Brayden that this had all been testing by Jessica. It was putting Selene through something she didn't need to go through. He growled and pushed Selene to the side. "Talk."

"I had to be confident about what the Council told me." Jessica backed away.

"Certain of what?" he hissed.

"Selene is a very rare type of shifter, a multatransfiguarian. They are created by the gods, gifted to the Earth. There are only five of them known to exist."

"Created?" Selene pushed him aside as she stood up to Jessica this time.

"You can't remember anything before waking up because there was nothing before you woke up."

"I've no mother or father?"

"No, but so little is known about your kind."

"My kind?" Her response was curt. Selene felt affronted, she may not know much about what she was but she knew she didn't like being referred to as a 'kind'.

"I'm sorry. I didn't mean that offensively."

"I know." Selene's shoulders slumped in defeat. "Who is this Council?"

Kas stood up to answer this question. "The Council are the group that governs all shifters and other non-humans around the world. They came into existence because of arguments between us that turned really nasty. Each pack was allowed to choose a representative. Any problems are decided democratically. The Council collect records for future generations, provide teaching to those that need it, and sanctuary as well. Due to the disputes, many shifters have lost their homes. They go to the Council and are placed with other packs." Kas' explanation of the Council seemed pretty simple and particularly polite for a man who would rather not deal with them.

"Why didn't they come for me when I was created?"

"That is a good question, and one I cannot answer." Jessica answered.

"What happens now? Can I go home with Jane?"

Selene was facing Kas again.

"I would advise against that."

"Why?"

Jessica was at her side. "The Council assures me that one day you will be able to control the powers you have. Learn the imprint of the creatures you touch and choose when to shift and return to your normal state. Until then, you are vulnerable."

"Vulnerable, like I could have touched Brayden in the middle of the café and exposed him?"

"There is that, but I mean vulnerable in the fact there will be lots of people seeking to take advantage of your powers for their own benefits."

"What, like Jessica just did to help me amplify hers?" Selene asked.

"Something like that."

"You want me to stay here so that you can protect me?"

"If you are in agreement, I believe that to be the best thing." Kas looked around to everyone in the back before settling his piecing stare back on Brayden.

"Am I staying as a prisoner or as a guest?" Selene raised an eyebrow in question.

"You will be an honorary pack member."

Brayden was shocked. Pack membership was normally like pulling teeth with Kas: painful, and it took forever. "What's the game, Kas?"

"There is no game, Brayden. I truly believe Selene to be in danger, and I want to help her."

"If I stay, I want some assurances." Selene's response was adamant. Brayden could see that she was not going to be fobbed off what she wanted out of this discussion.

"Tell me?" Kas bowed his head to show he was listening.

"I want freedom of movement. I will not be trapped in that little room while you wait for me to learn to control my powers."

"Of course. I'm sure Brayden will be willing to ensure that is enforced." Brayden nodded his agreement to Kas.

"And secondly, I want meetings set up with these other shifters. If I'm one of them, I want to know everything." Selene's lips had pursed together to show that she meant business. Brayden liked this display of strength.

"I will get Jessica to arrange it."

Selene turned her attention to his mother. "Do you think I'm doing the right thing?"

"At the start of the day I wouldn't have been so sure, but right now I believe that this is the safer option. And I have complete faith in Brayden being here as well." Jane replied.

The flicker of determination in Selene's eyes showed Brayden that she had made her decision. He held his breath.

"Ok, Kas. I will stay."

CHAPTER SIX

"You need to move quicker, Selene."

Quicker? What the hell! She was covered in sweat from moving as fast as she could. She ducked a kick that Emma had aimed at her head. It connected with her arm on the way down, causing golden fur to appear before returning to skin. "I'm mostly human remember, not a fucking cat. I don't have freaky abilities like you do."

"If you're part of the pack, then you'll need to fight like us." Brayden was frowning at her supposedly slow movements. He had his arms folded across his chest studying her every move. She jumped back from a fistful of claws that flashed past her face.

"Maybe I should start roaring and rubbing my backside against trees, as well? Show you just how much of a cat I can be."

Emma caught her in the face with the back of her paw, and she tumbled to the ground. Her eyes sparked into a feline's; her vision changing.

"Shit!" At the last minute, she rolled as a newly shifted Emma leaped for her.

Brayden snickered. She wanted more than anything to forget about the powerful lioness and smack him in the face instead. "When I'm done here you're going to owe me!" she growled.

"How do you figure that?"

"Because I'm going to win."

This time he bellowed out his laughter. "If that happens, then I'll be your slave for a month."

"Deal."

She watched as he stood up and shifted into his natural form. She'd once feared him as a snow leopard, but over the last month, she'd begun to find it the most fascinating thing in the world. She'd find herself spending hours just watching him move around. Brayden's distraction allowed Emma to get the better of her and she was pinned to the floor. She hated these lessons.

Being with Jessica was fun, and she enjoyed practicing the spells. She was becoming a little more controlled with them. There had been no more smashed chairs, though there was a rather large hole in the lounge wall where she had sent a ball of energy through it. Luckily, she'd missed Katia who was practicing her yoga exercises on the other side of it.

The fighting, however, was much harder and far more strenuous. They'd discovered that she was stronger than an average human which probably explained how she'd managed to bruise Brayden when she had struck out at him. She had quick reflexes but not as fast as those of the felines. It meant that when she was normally finished with these exercises, she was in dire need of a hot bath and a few strong painkillers.

Zain and Scott joined those watching the training session.

"Come on, Selene." The male lion called out, and Emma hissed at him.

"What? It'd be good to see you flat on your back for once." Brayden leaped at Scott, and the two started to tussle. Zain took a seat and commenced eating from a rather large pot of honey. He wasn't going to exert himself anytime soon. At least not until the pot was quite empty. That was one thing Selene had learned. The felines were full of energy while the bears and the wolf, Tyler, took things at a far more leisurely pace.

Emma, having been distracted by Scott, now refocused her attention on Selene. She lifted one paw and extended her claws. It was the first to draw blood who was considered the victor. It was about to happen again. Her losing. But that is when she saw it...

**

Selene disappeared.

Everyone froze, except Emma, who swiped her claws through the now empty muddy ground.

"Selene." Brayden had changed back to his human form. "Where the hell is she? How can she just disappear?"

Zain's nose appeared from the honey pot he had been licking and protectively hugged it to his chest. "If she's after my honey I won't be responsible for my actions."

A naked Selene suddenly appeared, touched Emma to grow claws and swiped at the lioness' fur. It stained with crimson blood. Selene had won.

She jumped up and down in celebration while Emma collapsed to the floor in defeat.

"How did you do that?" The lioness was stunned.

"Do what?" Selene tried so very hard to look perfectly innocent.

"Disappear!" Brayden pulled on his jeans and shirt while he spoke.

"Oh that. That was nothing, just a little magic."

He growled in response.

"Alright, Mr. Grumpy." She opened her tiny hand to reveal a squashed flea. "I think Emma might need a trip to the vet's."

Everyone collapsed onto the floor in fits of laughter. All except Emma, who turned bright red.

**

"You wanted to see me?" Jessica knocked on Kas' door and entered.

"Come in. How was the meeting?"

"It went well. I've got some reference books for Selene to help her understand and control the magic. How has she been?"

"She is experimenting more."

"Any control?"

"Not really. We've had lots of mishaps when she has been touched."

"She should be controlling her powers more by now."

"That is what I thought." Kas turned to a picture on his wall. Why did he still have it? It would be easier to just throw it in the bin or burn it, but somehow, he could never bring himself to do it.

Jessica must have followed his gaze. "The longer she has no control, the more dangerous she is to us all. Especially if Nuka finds her."

"He will come for her."

"What should we do?

"I've asked Brayden to double his guard. Take it in turns with Scott, Emma, and Tyler to ensure she is never alone."

"How has she taken that?"

"She was a bit confused when she was asked to move into Emma's room so Emma could do the night shift, but she did not argue. I just don't trust my brother. I know Nuka is plotting something. He's too quiet."

Kas sat back in his chair. "Brayden seems to be able to talk her into accepting our conditions."

"They appear to be getting very close." The concern was evident on the witch's face.

"They are. I was a little concerned at first, but it is good for Brayden."

"Do you think they are mates?" Jessica asked.

"I don't believe they can be anything until she learns to control her powers. There is a bond developing though. You saw him when he warned us she was his to protect."

"I did. Kas, there was something else. The Council gave me a spell to bind Selene's powers. Should we do it? Until we can work on the control."

He got up and went to the window. All the others had disappeared except for Selene and Brayden. Brayden had plastic gloves on and was rubbing cream over Selene's bruises. Their eyes met. He put his hand over a bruise, bent, and kissed it.

Brayden was a solitary animal. To share space with someone was against his very nature, but lately, Kas had noticed that every moment they seemed to be together.

The growing affection between them was evident despite their inability to touch skin to skin.

"I think we should leave things the way they are for now."

"You sure?"

"Selene has come to us for a reason. We need to work on her control issues. Once we find the key to that, in any coming storm that we have to survive she will give us a distinct advantage."

"I will accept your instruction. I just hope it is the right one." He knew the witch was worried. He was as well. He took one final look out of the window. Brayden helped Selene to her feet, her hands wrapped in long black gloves that she had taken to wearing. They strolled off together.

"So do I."

***

"Are you warm enough?" Brayden held another blanket out to Selene.

"Thank you." She still felt cold up in the mountains.

After the fight this morning, Emma had decided she needed to prove her worth. Selene, Scott, and Brayden had followed the lioness up the mountain. Emma's only interest was finding something, anything bigger than a goat and bringing it down for dinner.

They'd lit a fire and had a pan heating so whatever they caught Selene would be able to eat as well.

"I smell something. I think it's a bighorn. Let's go." Emma was shifted and ready before any of them could answer.

"You go, Scott. I'll stay with Selene."

"I was kind of hoping I could stay with Selene. It took it out of me walking up that mountain."

"No." Brayden glared at the lion. Selene tried to suppress her laugh.

Scott got to his feet and stomped off. She was pretty certain she heard him mumbling something about horny cats.

Selene took out a stick to prod the fire. "Did you bring

s'mores?"

"Is that a serious question?"

"Yes."

"Let's just say we're not chocolate people."

"That's it. I'm going back to California. You people are crazy. You make me fight all day and then don't give me chocolate to say you're sorry." She gave a fake pout.

"I'll go to the shops and get you lots of chocolate tomorrow. What else is in a s'more?"

She couldn't help it. He looked so serious about making sure she was happy, and she'd been teasing him. She rested her hand against his chest. He had a lightweight sweater on so their flesh did not touch. She let out a long breath.

"If I could tickle you right now I would." Brayden froze the second the words had left his mouth.

"I wish you could."

Selene had never wanted someone to touch her as much as she wished he could. He lifted his hand to her face and then stopped.

"Touch me." She pleaded.

She shut her eyes and an image of them writhing naked together flashed into her brain.

"I should go help Emma if we want to eat tonight. I'll send Scott back." When she opened her eyes, Brayden was already on the other side of the fire, his t-shirt over his head. He went for the button on his jeans but stopped and looked back at her. She couldn't take her eyes off him.

"Please." She sounded so tiny when she spoke.

"Selene." Brayden couldn't take his eyes off her chocolate orbs glistening with unshed tears. Selene's eyes lowered down his body to his jean clad groin. His breath faltered and his cock hardened. She wanted to see him naked, not for shifting purposes but for the man that he was.

"Please." She was pleading.

He undid the buttons and lowered the jeans down his marble thighs; his magnificent cock sprung hard from his jeans. The tip was glistening in the moonlight with pre-cum.

He was hard for her. He wrapped his hand around his length and started to stroke it. She followed unblinkingly. He was getting faster and faster. His breath hitched every time his hand slid over the end. She couldn't take her eyes off him. She bit her lip.

"Stop me." His voice was strained; he was doing the pleading this time.

"No. I want this." she replied honestly.

He threw his head back and let out a long moan as he came. His essence was squirting into his other hand. It was the single most heavenly sight she'd ever seen.

CHAPTER SEVEN

Swirls of dark clouds formed overhead; portents of fury of what would be a storm. Selene did not mind though as in California she had rarely seen clouds. The first time it had rained she'd run outside and stood looking skyward. The downpour had drenched her so much so that when Brayden found her, she had been shivering uncontrollably in the cold Montana air.

She thought she should probably head back, but her feet appeared to be rooted to the spot. Brayden would just have to warm her up. They were getting really close, and she knew she was developing feelings for him. She knew they were building up into something serious; especially after the incident up in the mountains. Many a time, they'd been millimetres from kissing only to realize that doing so would lead to her shifting at a most inappropriate and extremely frustrating time. She really wished she had more control over her powers, but nothing seemed to work. It was exhausting.

No one seemed to understand how she, or anyone for that matter, needed skin on skin touch. They all had it. All she felt was that she couldn't have something so fundamental to life and it was debilitating. Hopefully, she could figure it out, the sooner, the better. It was not only exhausting but bloody frustrating as well. She wanted so much to be able to explore a normal relationship with Brayden without the accompanying side effect that included growing a tail. It was a little inconvenient, mildly put.

The first few spots of rain started to fall. A rustling in the bushes broke her reverie and drew her attention. The white paw of a polar bear appeared as it lumbered out of the shadows. She'd learned that polar bears had special feet which meant that walking like it was very hard work. She'd studied Kas a few times in his human form, and sometimes the lazy step could be seen there as well.

"Hello, Kas."

The bear nodded in her direction as it sat in front of her and cleaned a paw. She was always a bit nervous of Kas, but he seemed relaxed today and settled at her feet as he continued to clean his paw.

"Been hunting?"

The bear nodded. The others seemed able to communicate in animal form, but this time Selene was already feeling as if she was having a one-way conversation.

"I see why it is necessary to have property in the middle of nowhere. Besides, it is a beautiful location."

The bear scratched behind his ear.

"Do you want me to find you some clothes so you can shift?"

The bear growled.

"Maybe I'll head back to the house." This time he shifted his weight and held out a paw. The rain was falling heavily now, and her little jacket wouldn't protect her much longer. "You want me to shift? I suppose I'll get less wet and be able to move more quickly. I'll need to keep a touch on you at all times. It's just that I haven't really changed fully since the incident with the flea."

The paw waved again.

She reached out and touched the bear. Her entire body shifted to grow fur and change into the animal before her. She felt no pain as she shifted, it was just like her body was meant to do it. Transformation completed, she looked around and gave a little growl. It felt good, she felt alive.

The rain pelted down but her fur-covered body did not feel it. She took a step forward and tumbled to the ground. Kas was still touching her. It was difficult adjusting to four legs when two was the norm. She laughed inwardly, but it still came out as some strange bear noise, sort of a cross between a growl and a snicker. This trying to be an animal was going to take some getting used to. She would have to practice with Brayden; Kas was scary. Mind you today he seemed to be having an exceptionally chilled day. Maybe he was drunk?

The bushes parted again, and a snarling pair of felines came out of them. Brayden and Emma, in shifted form, tails thickly agitated in anger, their fur primed for attack. Did they not recognize her? Surely that scent thing they were always talking about was still showing the second bear was her. After all, she wasn't a different person, just a different shape. Kas strengthened his grip on her. Brayden's growl deepened; his stance was ready to fight.

Tyler and Zain appeared next, shifted and ready to fight, also. The bushes crashed apart to reveal Kas in human form. He immediately moved in front of Brayden and Emma and stood in the front of the line of shifted clan members.

"Let her go Nuka. You know you will not be able to leave this land with her. She needs permanent touch to stay shifted." Kas commanded. Nuka? Who the hell was Nuka? "Let her go, and we will let you leave without a problem."

Brayden bared his sharply fanged teeth more.

"Brayden. No." Kas' order stopped the snow leopard, but she could see his desperation to get to her.

The world began to change again. Fur receded to be replaced with human skin. She realized the bear had let her go. Even before she was on her feet, she was crawling, as quickly as she could, towards Brayden, already in human form to take her into his care and protection.

She looked back at the polar bear who had held her. "Brother," Nuka called.

"You have a wolf, a bear, and a lioness ready to pounce on you. I suggest you remain where you are."

Nuka looked at the primed pack. "I take your point."

"Why are you here?" Kas queried

"I wanted to see the new shifter who is causing waves in our world."

"You should have made an appointment."

"Really? You would have shown her off?" Sarcasm dripped from Nuka's reply

"When she is ready, yes."

"You mean bent to your way."

"I mean when she wants to meet others." The tension was evident in Kas' voice. He wanted his brother gone from his lands. That scared Selene. It meant that she was in danger.

Nuka laughed. "You haven't even allowed her to fully shift. All her movements were those of a new changer. She is like a cub."

"Maybe she has chosen not to fully shift." Kas' eyes narrowed. "Why don't we ask her?"

The air was tense and full of power.

"You would trespass and risk death just to ask her if she has fully shifted before today?" Brayden growled in front of her.

"I would take great pride in being her first."

"Well, I am sorry to disappoint you but you are not her first." Brayden snarled.

Selene peeked out from behind Brayden's naked human torso. They were looking at her for confirmation. She nodded.

"Well, I guess you won't need Jessica's spells to control her powers then?"

"What?" Brayden spat out and glared at Kas.

"Oh dear. Have I said something that I shouldn't have?" Nuka didn't look the least bit remorseful. "I guess I should leave you to deal with that, dear brother. Selene, if you ever wish to talk about your abilities with somebody else, you are always welcome to visit the Banff Pack."

Nuka shifted back into a polar bear and left the group the way he'd come. Emma, Zain, and Tyler followed to make sure he left the property.

"Are you alright? Did he hurt you?" Brayden's jade eyes searched her for injuries. She couldn't help but feel self-conscious, she was completely naked and soaked by the rain.

Kas removed his jacket and put it around her shoulders.

"I'm fine. I was just shocked." She looked up at Kas, "I thought it was you."

"My identical twin. You are not the first he has fooled, and I doubt you will be the last."

"He needs to stay away from her. No more wandering alone because you will be with me at all times outside the house and in it."

"Brayden, you worry too much. He just wanted to see me shift."

"For his own purposes. And as for you." Brayden turned his attention to Kas. "What did he mean about spells?" There was genuine anger in his words.

"Now is not the time. Let's get Selene out of the rain." Kas dismissed Brayden's concerns.

"Not until you talk." Even stark naked, Brayden was intimidating.

"Jessica was given a spell by the Council when she visited them in Berlin recently. It can bind Selene's powers if she cannot learn to control them."

"Bind my powers?" She interrupted in shock.

"You would be normal. Humans and shifters alike could touch you with no reaction." Kas replied.

"Could it be reversed?" she asked.

"Only by the witch who performed the first ritual." Kas pointed towards the house.

"That is good to know."

"Are you considering this?" Brayden turned his anger towards her now.

"No."

"Good, this doesn't happen." He faced Kas. "Selene is getting more control every day."

"We should get inside." Kas again dismissed the conversation and wandered off towards the house.

If she were normal, she could touch people. There would be no hearing thoughts when she brushed up against someone or turning into some wild creature that got her shot. She could have a relationship with Brayden. She could touch him. Feel the warmth of his skin against hers. Normal. Normal.

CHAPTER EIGHT

She couldn't see their faces, but she sensed that they loved her. The room was filled with adoration as they watched her kick tiny feet and wave chubby little hands. She was a baby. Settled and peaceful. The mother reached out and touched her, no thoughts, no shifting. Just contentment.

The mood changed. Sadness and sorrow filled the air; weeping cascaded through her head. The mother and father no longer happy but grieving beside an empty cot.

She woke with a start. Her body was clammy and heart beat rapidly.

"Selene." Brayden was there. "What happened? You were screaming."

"A nightmare." He handed her a drink of water, and she took a sip.

"Do you want to talk about it?" Concern laced his words.

"It was strange. I more sensed everything rather than saw it. I was a baby with two loving parents, and then they were grieving because I was gone." She felt really sad.

"You think it was a memory?"

"It felt like one." She shrugged.

"Jessica said you were created, though. You weren't born."

"I know." She lay back down on the bed. It was so confusing. "My mind, just playing tricks on me. The meeting with Nuka, my powers, and the feelings I am developing for you, it's all made me really tired."

"Feelings for me?"

"Is that all you heard from what I said?"

"Pretty much." He chuckled. "So these feelings?"

"I like you." She was embarrassed now; her cheeks heating.

"In what way?"

"Brayden, you know how I feel. Unless I've been severely mistaken after that day on the mountain, I think you feel it too. But it can never be. We can't even touch each other." She looked down at the bed, wishing it would swallow her up and take away all the fears that she had.

"I would love nothing more than to be intimate with you, to feel myself moving inside you, making love to you. But, you're right. It's not possible. That doesn't mean however that we cannot express the feelings we have for each other. Do you trust me, Selene?"

"I've trusted you since the moment I first met you, even with the whole scary snow leopard in the middle of Death Valley thing."

"You'll be bringing that up when we are old, won't you?"

"Of course. Would you prefer me to refer to it as that pussycat thing?" She stuck her tongue out at him.

"Have you ever been intimate with someone?"

Selene shook her head.

"Have you touched yourself? Do you know the pleasure your body can bring you?"

She suddenly wanted to bury her head under the sheets and die. Touch was such a big issue to her, she shied away from all forms of it. Even with herself.

"No." Her voice was tiny.

The mewl of desire that came from the back of Brayden's throat sent shivers through her body, causing her breath to hitch.

"We will take this very slowly then. "

"You can't take me, my virginity. I will change."

"That is something we will work on with your control. But for now, I just want to learn the most trivial and intimate details of your body. Not everything sexual is just going for it. Remove your clothes. I want to see you, all of you."

"You have seen all of me before."

"That was different. This is for me to learn your curves, the way your breasts fall, the color of your nipples when you are excited. I want to smell your desire for me. I want to see your clit swell with lust for me."

It was her turn to let out a soft moan of desire.

She swung off the bed and stood beside it. Brayden was in jeans, his muscular chest proudly displayed and beautiful in its definition, each line like some Ancient Greek statue. She bit her lip as a thought crossed her mind.

"What are you thinking?"

"Nothing."

"Selene."

"One day, I want to lick the muscles of your torso."

"Oh God." He reached down and unbuttoned his jeans. "Clothes off, now."

She only had her PJ's on, so it was easy and quick to remove them and leave her standing naked before him. He let out a growl of appreciation. His cat-like eyes darkened to a rich emerald. His jeans were off and thrown across the room before she had a chance to let out another breath.

She felt like prey about to be devoured by the ferocious beast, but this time it was a good feeling, an exquisite feeling.

"I can smell your arousal; you like me looking at you."

"I do. I feel attractive under your gaze."

"Put your finger between your legs and show me the wetness."

"I.." She hesitated.

"I cannot touch you down there because I'm terrified that I won't be able to stop and that I will hurt you. We can make love in animal form, but that is not what I want for your first time because it will not be the same for you. Animals mate for procreation, not for love. Especially snow leopards." Slowly, almost unconsciously, she moved her hand down her body and between her thighs. She touched the cleft between her legs. She was soaked with her own essence. Something sparked when she went over a particularly sensitive spot, her clit.

She groaned long and hard as she touched the spot again.

"Show me your fingers."

So very reluctantly, she eased her hand away and held it up. Her fingers glistened with her juices.

Brayden dipped forward and took in a long breath. "I know that your hand will change, but I must taste you. Please, may I lick your fingers?"

"Yes. Please, please do it."

His mouth wrapped around her fingers, his tongue had all the hallmarks of a cat, agile and slightly rough to the touch. She started to shift, the tingle that also accompanied it ricocheting all over her body. Her head fell back, eyes closed, and she let out a cry. She could barely stand it, such was the heightened perception all through her body. Brayden let go and whipped a sheet from the bed. He wrapped it around her just as her legs gave way. Tenderly he placed her on the bed and pulled the sheet away.

"What happened?" He asked.

"When I change it sends a feeling through my body. I don't know why, but it was so very, very intense this time."

"May I touch you again?"

"Yes." She lay back and shut her eyes, focusing on Brayden's gentle touches as he lightly rubbed his fingers over her body in soft strokes. Each one was no longer than a second long but the sensation stayed with her longer and longer. He stopped. She opened her eyes and found him stroking himself in front of her.

"I have to stop touching you, or I'm going to lose control."

"I want to taste you."

"You can't."

"This is so unfair."

"Ssh. It is what must be for now. It will not be forever." The light dimmed in his eyes for the briefest of seconds, but it was enough to let her know he was worried that it would. "I'm going to place the sheet between us. I will move as though I'm making love to you, but I will bring myself to climax. I want you to do the same. I won't last long. It has been a while."

"Brayden, I'm scared."

"What of?"

"Touch. My emotions and touch seem so off key with each other. What if something happens when I reach that moment. What if I can't reach that moment?"

"Moment?" He questioned; the concern etched on his face.

"Climax." She bit her lip with the worry.

"I will be here the entire time with you. Nothing is going to happen."

"We don't know that though, we don't know anything about me."

"I know you. I know that you are the sweetest woman I've ever met; you have a heart of gold mixed with the perseverance of any feline I've ever known. You've got a wicked sense of humor and a killer body that has me hard and ready to explode even when you are wearing clothes and when you are not, well . . . What else do you want to know?"

"That I'm not going to literally make you explode when I come."

"If you do, we will deal with it or I will have died with a smile on my face thinking I was already in heaven." He replied with a wicked grin. "Lay back, switch that mind of yours off. Just concentrate on feelings." She did as he said as he placed the sheet over her. Slowly, over the white cotton, he started to kiss down her body. She shut her eyes again. Sensuous tremors flooded her body.

"Imagine, Selene," he reminded her. She focused on his lips, in her mind, they were not on the sheet, but her body. His tongue flicking a nipple to a stiff peak. It ached, so she fondled it herself. He caressed her clit through the sheets.

"More, please," she pleaded desperately.

He returned his hand and pressed harder this time. Selene wanted to come; she needed to come. Brayden moved his hand away again, causing her to whimper.

"Too eager." He placed the sheet over her mouth and moved his lips. They were kissing. He was showed devoted care not to touch any of her flesh.

Brayden lay over her and Selene felt something between her thighs. She realized it was his rock-hard penis. He was moving as if making love to her but constrained only by the barrier of the sheet. She could feel him stroking against her clit, an animalistic urgency taking over. She knew he wouldn't stop this time. His hand twisted against her nipple again, and she came apart with a cry of animalistic pleasure. Her whole body started to shake, never was the feeling that she was experiencing something she had ever expected. She was screaming his name, everyone would know what they were doing, but she didn't care. At that moment, it was her and her lover, Brayden. She bit down on his lip through the sheet when he moved hard against her again. She came again, harder, more intense. Brayden growled, as she felt his body shudder over hers. The sheet dampened between them as he came, and the familiar tingle started. She couldn't move, she was changing just from the touch of his essence. He must have sensed the shift in her as he ripped the sheet from her body and threw it across the room. He grabbed and blanket and wiped her dry.

"Wait." She called.

"What?"

She looked down to see the fur receding from her pelvic region. "You tasted me. I want to eat you."

"Selene, you shifted just from having my cum on you."

"Please. I have to try." A single tear tumbled down her cheek in a slow wavering path.

"It will happen. I promise you." He pulled the sheet away and threw it on the floor. From Emma's bed, he pulled a fresh one and wrapped it around her. She just lay there, her mind a whirlwind of emotions. Touch was ugly, touch was evil, but she'd just learned that it could also be the most amazing thing in the world. It was something she'd never have again unless she found how to take control over her abilities. Brayden pulled her close. She wanted to hold him and make love to him again, correctly this time.

"Did this make things worse?" Brayden was scared of her answer.

"No, it just made me realize that I need to do whatever I can to get my powers under control."

"We'll double our effort tomorrow. Maybe we are looking at it the wrong way. We are trying to control your ability to shift." He settled on the bed next to her and put his hand on her stomach over the sheet. "Maybe we should have you shift and control from there."

"I'm up for trying anything at this point." There was great sadness in her voice.

"Why don't you try and get some more sleep. I won't leave you."

"You need to sleep as well." Selene queried.

"I'll catch up later."

"In other words, you don't want to fall asleep and risk touching me."

"I'll sleep in the chair." He threw his weight off the bed and moved back to the chair that he used as his guarding post.

Selene had just experienced the single most pleasurable and erotic moment of her life. She knew the feelings that she had for Brayden were more than just on the surface. She was being pulled to him, the connection between them becoming stronger every day. Why then did she feel more alone than ever before?

CHAPTER NINE

"Selene." The soft rocking woke her from dreams of normality with Brayden.

"Am I having a nightmare again?" she mumbled sleepily.

"Not that I'm aware of, you appeared to be sleeping well."

"Kas?"

That voice, it was too formal to be Brayden. It didn't have the Montana twang. No, it sounded more like Kas, he always tried to hide the Inuit roots in his accent. But that would be silly? Why would Kas be in her bedroom? Why would he be trying to wake her? She was definitely dreaming.

"Selene, I need you to wake. It's time to make the decision about your future."

She sat up and rubbed her eyes.

"May I talk frankly?" Kas asked. She wasn't dreaming.

"Of course." She took a sip of water that she'd left on the bedside table. That would wake her up.

"Brayden has gone off up the mountain. He does that when something is worrying him."

"You heard us earlier." She felt ashamed.

"Yes. I'm afraid our hearing is excellent, it's a hazard in this house."

"I'm sorry." She blushed.

"You have nothing to be sorry about. What you both want is natural. We all see that you are meant to be mates." His reply was said with great honesty.

"Yet, fate conspires against us so that we can't even touch."

"I believe Brayden taught you that touch is not everything."

"But wanting the touch of snow is." The words flowed from her mouth with sorrow lining every syllable.

"And that is why you need to make a decision." He perched on the end of the bed. "Your powers are still erratic. You still have no control over them."

"I thought I was getting some, but they are still all over the place and it's causing danger. I'm terrified to leave your property. What if I were to touch one of the pack in the street with humans about? Even worse, what if someone I don't know touched me when we were out, and they happened to be some other non-human? If I changed, it would reveal everyone to the world." She shivered. "I cannot live this way my entire life, though. It was alright when I thought only humans existed and I could hide the thoughts." She paused. "You woke me to do the spell while he is gone, didn't you?"

"If that is what you choose, I will not force you. I'm worried about your shifting abilities in public. The summer season is picking up, and soon the visitors to the park will increase. I would be reluctant to allow you off my land or even a small distance from the house. As a pack leader, I have to do what I must to protect everyone in the pack. Even if it means placing restrictions on a pack member."

"We are not talking about binding my powers forever, are we? I was created for a reason. I believe that."

"No, I will continue to work with you, and Jessica will continue to liaise with the Council to try to find a way to control them. She can release the spell anytime she wishes and replace it again." He turned away from her, the full moon of the night flooding in her window. She could feel the sadness surrounding him. "I know what it is to deny what you are for so long; to have gifts but not be able to share them with the world."

"I would say you are talking about your ability to shift, but I feel there is more."

"I once loved someone, a woman I believed to be my mate. She was beautiful and enigmatic. She was my gift; she made me a better person, a better leader. I wanted to show her off to the world as my wife one day, but I had to set her free to save her from a fate she could not have lived with."

"What happened to her?"

"She married another and started a family. She was happy."

"I'm sorry. I can see she meant a lot to you."

"She always will." He bristled like he was shaking his fur and the feeling of sorrow from his body. "That is why I want to give you and Brayden a chance to have what I never did. Whatever the reason you have these powers we will discover it, but in the meantime, you can be normal."

"Normal is what I dream of."

"Jessica is downstairs, she is prepared and ready to do the spell if that is what you choose. We'll be waiting in my office."

"Kas," She reached out and touched his hand, her body instantly starting to shift. "Pass me my robe please. I want to do it."

***

Brayden had shifted to a snow leopard the second he left the house, his big fluffy feet and razor-sharp claws propelling him further up the mountain. Jumping from rock to rock, some as far as fifty feet away. This was when he was at his most peaceful: alone, as dawn approached. A rabbit caught his eye, and he pounced. It was a little snack to give him the energy to climb back down the mountain. After devouring his catch, he sat and cleaned himself. He always took pride in his white fur.

He wondered if Selene would clean him in snow leopard form. His beautiful Selene.

He leaped to his feet and started back down the mountain. Prey scattered in front of him but he was not interested, his only thought to get back to the angel he'd left sleeping. He shifted back to his human form at the front door and took the stairs two at a time. If he woke anyone, so what? Lazy buggers could do with getting up early. He was in love. He did, however, push the door to her bedroom open quietly. He wanted to watch her wake slowly, not in fright. Her eyelids fluttering open and looking at him with a hazy recollection before focusing and realizing he was there for her. The early rays of dawn were starting to flood into the room.

The bed was empty. He'd left Kas on guard, and he wasn't there either. In an instant, he was running back down the stairs,

"Selene?" He inhaled deeply, she had walked this way recently. He followed the scent to Kas' office. What was going on?

He thrust the door open in a fury.

***

"Akasha binding, Goddess restricting, Grant this spirit's release."

The flash of white light held her floating in the air before dropping her down to her to the floor. Jessica's eyes returned to normal.

"It is done." She too collapsed, the power of the magic she had used rendering her momentarily weak.

"Selene?" Brayden's voice filled the room. He stood in the doorway. "What have you done?"

"Give them a moment." Kas stepped forward.

"You bound her powers?" Brayden yelled out.

"It was her choice." Jessica's reply was short and to the point.

"You forced her to do it when I was away. What lies did you spin her?" Brayden pulled his fist back and sent it slamming into Kas' face. The polar bear did not move.

"No. Stop it. It was my choice." Selene called out and

tried to stand. Her legs were still weak from the spell. "I want to be normal." Her wobbly legs took her over to Brayden. His fists were still balled and ready to lash out but they gradually relaxed. "Kiss me. Please."

"You did this for us?"

"Yes." She couldn't wait any longer, she had to touch him. She leaned in and pressed her lips against his, they were soft, but the stubble on his face reminded her that he was all man. It was perfect. No thoughts entered her head from his mind, no fur...no fur.

Her body started to tingle.

No. No. It couldn't be happening. She was changing. She felt the hair growing down from her lips, her neck, across her shoulders and lower. No. No. This wasn't supposed to happen. Brayden released and pulled away.

"It didn't work." Kas looked at them in shock. Her body shifted back to human.

"I don't understand." Jessica was frantically checking her notes and all the magical paraphernalia on the floor. "Everything was done right."

"We can't touch." Brayden's voice was broken. He'd stepped back from her, the distance between them again. How could they be mates when they couldn't be intimate?

"You told me this would work!" She turned on Kas. "You said that I could have a life. You knew this would happen. You lied." She'd never been a violent person, but something inside of her snapped. She lashed out at Kas, a rapid succession of punches to his face and body. "Make it work! Make it work!"

"Selene!" Jessica's loud call stopped her mid punch. "You're not changing."

"What?" Selene looked down at her hand, Kas' astonished gaze was on it as well. She should have a polar bear paw, but she had only a human hand. "I'm not changing." She placed her hand on Kas' bare arm. Nothing happened. "I don't understand."

"Jessica?" Kas had no answers either. Selene hoped the

witch would.

"Touch Brayden again, maybe it took a few seconds to work?" Jessica held her hands out in a fumbling explanation.

Brayden rushed for her, but the second they touched she started to shift to a snow leopard.

"No, no, no!" Brayden cried out. He pulled back again and shrank into the corner of the room, as far away from her as he could possibly get.

"The others." Selene remembered the other members of the pack and fled the room. Brayden, Jessica, and Kas were following closely as she broke into Zain's room. The black bear was sound asleep with a pot of honey tucked under his arm. Selene touched him, nothing. Next was Scott's room. They found him wrapped around a lioness who was busy taking care of his morning wood.

"What the fuck? Get out!"

"Shut up. We'll only be a minute." Brayden venomously responded. Selene touched Scott, but nothing happened. She even touched the skanky lioness, but the same occurred, nothing, no shifting. The story was no different with Katia, Emma, and Tyler. Every time she didn't change. It was only with Brayden. She slumped down to the floor in the hallway bringing her legs up to her chest in defeat.

"I made the wrong decision. I tried to change who I am. This is my punishment: to never touch the man, I love."

"I'll do the spell again. Maybe I did something wrong?" Jessica knelt down beside her.

"No, it will be the same outcome. It will always be the same. Brayden and I can never touch as humans. That is our destiny.

"I won't accept that." The loud growl echoed through the high-ceilinged room.

"We have no choice." She was defeated.

"You're going to give up?" Brayden said.

She nodded.

Without so much as a word, Brayden shifted and left.

CHAPTER TEN

"Lynx, bring me some breakfast, and make sure it's seal blubber." Nuka had been out all night with a group of whores, and now he was in a foul mood. He stormed through the corridors of the Banff Pack's expansive cabin towards Ciaran's room. He kicked the door open. The place stank of herbs again. He was sure Ciaran just had them around to annoy him. They didn't seem to serve much purpose. Yesterday had gone well but whenever he saw his self-righteous brother it always resulted in a bad mood. The hangover and poorly sucked dick didn't help, either.

"Nuka," His Druid warlock and Beta greeted him. His room was strewn with magical books and paraphernalia. Ciaran was his right-hand man, and he trusted him implicitly. Ciaran was more powerful than most people imagined. "Did your mission go well?"

"If you are asking whether or not I put the spell on the girl, then yes. It was transferred when I touched her and she shifted." Nuka grumpily replied.

"Did she react in any way to it?" The wizard placed the spell book down that he held and focused on him.

"Not that I noticed. That was a good plan of yours, to transfer the magic by her shifting." He chuckled.

"Your brother is a mistrusting man. That makes him vulnerable to the underhanded type of attack because he is too focused on the obvious. You'll need to kill the snow leopard first, for our plan to work though. She has to be at her weakest and want to give up her powers before my spell will work."

"I never had the misguided affection for him that my brother seems to have. It won't be a problem." Nuka shut his eyes. "What happens now. I'm impatient. I want her powers."

"I'm afraid we have to wait for Jessica to put the binding spell on Selene, it's the only way I can see the plan working." His warlock cackled. "She will be prevented from shifting for everyone bar Brayden. We swoop in and play the heroes. Remove my spell so she can touch the snow leopard without changing. Then the fun can begin."

Nuka settled into a chair, feet propped up on the stool next to it. Lynx strode in, dressed for a run. She laid the tray of food over his lap.

"Is there anything else?" She pursed her lips together in seductively.

"No, although I'd like you in my bed later," he growled.

"Say please," Lynx teased.

"Say 'do you want to find somewhere else to live?'" Lynx, and others like her, were what they termed a 'maid' to the pack. They had two others as well. Their basic duty was to ensure that the male shifters' priorities were all met.

"I'll do my run and then I'll be waiting for you."

"Bring Shauna and Lily as well. After last night, I want women that know what they are doing."

Lynx left them alone with a shake of her backside. Yes, he would enjoy tapping that later.

"Your brother sees him as key to the pack's continued success," Ciaran continued, unfazed by the sexual liaison being planned.

"Brayden's father was my brother's beta. When he died, Brayden took his place. He is only a hybrid though, not pure blood. He will be weak and destroy the pack. There are better people to lead it."

"Like you?"

"Amalgamate the two packs, and we will contain most of Montana and Banff. We can head out West and East, defy the Council and take over the lands that were once taken from us. Show ourselves to the human faction and rule the Americas, if not the world." Nuka banged his fist down on the table next to his chair.

"World domination?" Ciaran was always on board with his plans, if a little skeptical about them coming to fruition.

"Taking back what is rightfully mine."

"You never did tell me about your grandfather. What happened?"

"It seems like a lifetime ago. I was ten. The twenty-six years since then have aged me. My family owned lands in Idaho, Wyoming and Montana south of here and Alberta, Nunavat and Saskatchewan above. Nunavat is the part that hurts the most, that was our ancestral lands. That was where our forefathers roamed wild in their natural form. Though the Inuit blood has diffused into a more western genetic thanks in part to the diversification of the southern breeds. Our pack was always mixed. We were not elitist. A hybrid of two shifters is a lot better than one of a human and animal, so no humans were allowed. If you took one as a mate, then you left the pack. It was when they elected the first human-cheetah hybrid on the Council that things started to change for everyone. He didn't like the amount of land that we, my grandfather, was responsible for. We'd won that land fair and square, not just through fights but also through marriages. My own mother's lands in Glacial Park came into my grandfather's hands with her marriage to my father. I guess that is why Kas has it now. He always was a mommy's boy." The snigger that left his mouth showed the contempt that he had for his brother.

"Surely the Council couldn't take it away if you could prove it as being yours? In Scotland, the Council wanted my family seat shared with distant cousins in New Zealand. Their territory had been encroached on by the humans, and it was impossible for them to practice magic anymore. They could not take the land, though. It was fairly won and maintained by us. Handed down by the rules. We agreed to give my cousin's family a home and a place within the inner magic circle. But they would not rule in our place."

"No, they couldn't just take it. He was the ruler of the lands in all legal ways. A war of words started with the

Council but that war turned physical. A significant number of shifters died protecting what was theirs, but the Council eventually won. They killed my father and grandfather within days of each other."

"And that is when Kas took over?"

"Yes, he is the elder by a matter of minutes."

The warlock passed him a drink of malt whiskey. He downed it in one mouthful, the burning liquid tempering his anger so that he could finish his tale.

"Kas and my mother met with the Council. I was ordered to stay behind; such was my rage against the deaths. They brokered a deal which would stop the bloodshed but meant breaking up our lands." He said bitterly. "Idaho went to my cousins, the Evans; they had always sat on the fence during the fighting and were rewarded with riches. Wyoming and Saskatchewan went to the Council who split them between several tribes; all of whom were loyal to the Council. My brother gave me Alberta; he knew I had an affiliation with it since I had been young. I was to be hemmed in by the Holland's in Jasper Park though." He turned and spat at the floor. "Kas took Montana and retained a small proportion of Nunavut, where our families are buried. The rest was given over to a pack of polar bears who had formed during the fighting to protect the lands there from damage. The Council will not win. I'll rule one day as my grandfather did. I'll get back what is rightfully his." On that he was adamant. Kas was weak, he was strong. He would be King.

Nuka slammed the glass down on the table next to him. It shattered into a myriad of razor sharp pieces, but he simply shifted his hand to a bear's claw to protect his skin.

Ciaran waved his hand and the glass reformed and settled down on the table in front of them.

"Your brother is a traitor to his people. He's a coward who would not continue the fight. He will suffer for his treason. We'll see to that."

"I'm lucky to have found you, my friend." There was

genuine warmth in his affectionate words.

"We should thank the witch for that."

"Oh yes, your ex-lover, Jessica. She won't sense your spell on the girl?" He questioned.

"No, my magic far exceeds her abilities. She could've been the greatest, but she gave that up for your brother's pack. A mistake she will rue when I strip her of all her abilities and cast her into the realm of nothing for eternity."

"Sounds a cheery place." Nuka could feel the sullen mood lifting. There was nothing like planning revenge to lighten his spirits.

"I can send your brother there as well."

"Oh no, I have a much better plan for him. One that involves lots of pain for his betrayal. Pass me another whiskey. I feel the need to celebrate."

Before his Beta could do so, his eyes turned white and rolled into the back of his head. Nuka took the flask from the comatose Druid, poured his own whisky, and resumed his seat while he waited.

Eventually, the Druid returned to the here and now.

"Jessica is as predictable as ever." Ciaran mercilessly laughed. "The spell is done. The girl is vulnerable. They are ready for the taking.

"Good. That is certainly something to drink to." He held his glass up. Revenge would be his, and it'd change the face of the shifter world forever.

CHAPTER ELEVEN

Brayden slumped and shifted back to his human form. He wasn't sure how long he'd been running, but he was near the Harrison Glacier, his place of peace and tranquillity in the frozen hills. It was where he could be alone and silent. A few tourists walked the trail, but the majority left him to the shadows.

He should find one of the packs of his clothes that he left lying around for emergencies, but he just didn't have the energy to move. No, it wasn't a lack of energy it was a lack of motivation. Whatever previous life he had lived, the gods of nature must really hate him.

He rolled onto his back and felt the sun warm his face. If he lay here long enough, maybe he would melt like the ice around him; slowly eroding over decades.

"You better have lotion on that pale skin of yours, or you'll burn in no time. It's not tough like my old puma skin." Miss Molly's voice entered his head and the shadow of a puma came over him. She was a part of their pack, but not one they saw often. She spent all her time high in the mountains in her natural form. She had been involved in the fighting with Kas' grandfather and lost her leg. She preferred to be shifted as she said that it was easier to be on three legs rather than one. He had to admit she was kind of sprightly still and when she ran, you wouldn't even know she had only three legs.

"I'll roll over again in an hour. Should prevent burning in anywhere I don't want it."

"I don't know. The place I'm worried about could get a lot closer to the sun if you keep thinking of that cute girl of yours."

"Miss Molly!"

"What? You're a big lead. Just like your father was."

"I don't need to think of him that way, thank you." Brayden cringed.

"I remember many a time catching him after your mother up here. For a human, she could move pretty fast. It was impossible for him to hide how much he loved that woman even with his two big hands. He was a great man. It wasn't right what happened to him. Nuka had no business..." She trailed off.

"Nuka had no business what?" He sat up sharply; suddenly motivated.

"Nothing."

"Tell me!" he demanded.

"Nuka had no business being on Kas' lands that day." She frowned as she spoke.

"Did he kill my father?" That seemed to be the question that he was endlessly asking people.

"It is not as simple as one person killing your father. What happened that day runs so much deeper. You must understand that. When the time is right to tell you, Kas will."

"I don't see why I have to be kept in the dark." All he ever found was frustrating answers when it came to his father's death.

"It is safer that way. Kas may control these lands, but he is still governed by the Council." She paused. "Let's go to my cave. I have an excellent venison stew cooking. I'll share it with you. And you can tell me why you are hiding away up here."

"You caught a deer?"

"No, Tyler brought it for me yesterday. He's such a good boy."

"I'm sorry Miss Molly." He waved off her hand and stood. "I've neglected my duty."

"No you haven't, you found your mate and needed to help her."

"And on that, I've failed."

"What you see is different from what I see."

"What do you mean?"

"Food first."

Molly's cave was not really what one would expect. There were no damp walls and cold rock formations. No, the inside was like a palace. When she'd told Kas that she wanted to stay high up in the mountain, he had had them all turn her dwelling into a proper home. The inside was divided into rooms with as many modern conveniences as one could have. Electricity was provided by an ongoing spell Jessica had put in place.

Molly may be eccentric, but she lived like a Queen. The now in human form, puma grabbed a bowl and ladled a spoonful of the stew into it.

"Here get that inside you. It's my great-grandmother's recipe, handed down from generation to generation. This is older than Queen Victoria herself, I'll have you know."

He sat at her carved oak table. The Ming dynasty china bowl and silver spoon felt really delicate in his big hands. One wrong move and everything would end up smashed or bent.

"Stop staring at it and eat. Then you can tell me about your girl."

He took a mouthful, and it was delicious. Warmth slid down his throat in a mix of herbs and sauce. He purred his response.

"That good?" She laughed at him.

"You're a great cook, Miss Molly."

He quickly scooped more spoonfuls until the bowl was empty. It was just what he'd needed to bring back some level of rational thought.

"Did you ever want to take a mate, Miss Molly?" He wasn't sure where that thought had come from but he really wanted to know. It was said that she was alone up here.

"I thought about it once. There was a human, but then the war in Vietnam started, and he had to ship out. He saw things he couldn't live with. It changed him and destroyed us. As a shifter I would never know peace. I walked away from him and never saw him again. I heard he married a human female and had two children. I just hope that he was happy."

"Did you have a normal relationship up until he left for the war?"

"Do you mean was he aware of my abilities? Or intimacy?"

"I guess a bit of both."

"He accepted what I could be and even helped out in the pack. Kas' grandfather liked him but was obviously worried when we split. Albert assured him that the secret of our existence would die with him. He owed it to the love he still had for me. As for intimacy, we had a healthy relationship. It is important for both human and shifter to have that."

"It's important for a shifter and super shifter as well," he huffed out.

"I feared this when I saw the girl for the first time. She is not controlling her powers?"

Brayden shook his head.

"Worse than that. Jessica bound them, and it worked for everyone bar me. When she touches me, she still shifts. That is why I'm up here. I ran away. How can I find my mate and have this happen? What kind of cruel twist of fate is it?"

"I don't know about the twist of fate, but she is younger than any super shifter I've ever seen before. All have been male as well."

"You've met them? Even Jessica hasn't done that, and she's been researching them for a month." He sat up a bit straighter in his chair.

"Miss Molly has met a lot of people in her life Brayden."

"Where? When? How? I've so many questions."

"The first one I met in the summer of nineteen fifty-five, I was a girl of only six, so I don't remember it entirely. Hayden came to visit with my parents. He and my father had been roommates during the Second World War. I just have these visions of him changing into all these different animals in our back garden. I was so excited and clapping all the time, screaming out an animal for him to be. I think he even managed a dragon at one point, although not a unicorn. I was most disappointed at that." As she spoke, Molly ladled out another bowl of the stew for him, and he happily started to eat.

"A dragon? How? I thought their bodies learned from touching animals? And as far as we know dragons are extinct."

"Apparently, it works with bones as well. It's a cool thing to have up your sleeve. A fabulous display of fiery breath as well." He let his spoon rest on the edge of his bowl. He could see Selene as a dragon. She would be a beautiful white one with chocolate eyes. With her mischievous sense of humor as well he was sure that she would try to scare him, to get him back for Death Valley.

"What happened to him? Do you know where he his? Maybe we can meet him and get some answers for Selene."

"I wish that was possible. He died shortly after the visit."

"How?"

"Nobody knows; everybody suspects, but no one can find the truth. All we know is that he was mortally wounded by an animal. My father was devastated. He was never quite the same afterward. I think they had developed a bond akin to brothers."

"I'm sorry. Selene would be as well. Anyone who has the abilities that she does would be family to her."

Molly stood, using the furniture and a stick, to hop over to a comfortable armchair.

"You carry on eating. Those chairs are hard on my old bones. I prefer the softer one." She pulled a blanket over herself. He wanted to tuck it around her to ensure she was warm. She wouldn't like the fuss, though.

"You said that you had met more than one."

"Yes, Ethern. He is on the Council although I think he is more of a silent member now. I met him just after he was elected. When I was injured, he was the one who rescued me. Brought me back to Kas. He tried to multiply Jessica's powers so that my leg could be saved, but it didn't work. It was too badly damaged."

"I need to get Selene in to see him." There was hope after all, maybe this Ethern could help them.

"That will not happen."

"Why?" The flames of hope were rapidly doused.

"He is a recluse. When he found me it was after the fight in which Kas' grandfather died. He became disgusted with what he saw and knew what was happening with the Council. That is why he joined it, to bring stability. He brought about the end of the fighting in negotiating the deal with Kas."

"If Kas knows him, then surely we can try and meet him. I wonder why he hasn't sent Jessica to see him? She was in Berlin recently." He needed to get back down the mountain and question Kas. Why was the Polar bear dragging his heels on something that could help Selene?

"I don't know. Kas has his own rules that none of us really understand. He does what is best for his pack, but it may not always seem the most logical decision. There will be a reason. Again, you must trust him."

"This is all I seem to hear at the moment." He got to his feet and put his bowl into the sink. "Trust Kas, he knows what he is doing," he said sarcastically. The china clattered down and smashed. "Damn it!" He thumped the side of the cave.

"You really love her, don't you?"

"I do. I have visions of us running around with cubs like a proper family, I want to be with her all the time. To know that she is at my side and protected. I want to stroke her face and know that she feels my touch of love, not a touch that transforms her body." He slumped against the wall, a figure of defeat. "I can't even taste her lips because the second our mouths meet she turns. Her scent is driving me crazy, I can smell it all over me. I need her to be my mate in every sense of the word but it's not happening. It won't ever happen. Even if she gets control over her powers will she be able to touch me? They bound her abilities to everyone but me."

"It is mother nature's way Brayden. You have to understand that. She has put you both in this position for a reason. I know not what it is. I wish I could stand here and tell you, but I can't. All I know is that you have your father's strength and determination. You have his ability to love Selene as Heath loved Jane. Everyone sees it, we can all feel it when you walk into a room. You have a power about you. You've been destined for your father's life for so long, I think you've forgotten who you are. Find that. It will give you the answers you seek."

He strode forward and knelt before Miss Molly, his head bowed, hands in her lap.

"Thank you."

CHAPTER TWELVE

This used to be Selene's favorite burger, but it just tasted like cardboard now. Her appetite had gone, replaced with only a nauseated feeling that seemed like it would never leave. Kas had brought her back to California to be with Jane.

"Selene, please, you have to eat something." Jane's reassuring voice urged her on. She took another bite. Part of her wished Kas had just left her alone in her room to wallow after Brayden disappeared, but when he said he would bring her to see Jane she jumped at the chance to get away. Jane touched her hand, and Selene didn't flinch away. The spell was still in place so nothing would be felt.

"You need to keep up your strength. Brayden likes a bit of meat on his women."

The burger stuck in her throat and tears started to fall from her eyes.

"Oh, honey. I didn't mean to upset you. I can't imagine what you are feeling, but it will be alright. You'll find a way. Everyone is working on it; reading, researching, talking to contacts."

She looked down at her hand. Every time, she saw it shift to snow leopard skin. It wasn't, of course, because she was nowhere near Brayden. He'd run off and left her. She sighed heavily and swallowed the choking bite.

"I know it is so hard. When you love someone so much, you just want to be with them all the time." Memories of past times were reflected in Jane's words.

"Is that what you felt for Brayden's father?" Selene asked.

"Heath and I loved each other a great deal. He was my first and only lover. We were so young, so optimistic of a future filled with a large family and so much joy."

"You only had Brayden?"

"I was very young when I had him. There were complications, and I couldn't have any more children. We probably spoiled my son far too much as a result. We catered to his moods. Snow leopards are solitary animals, even though Brayden is half human he still has that side in him. Heath did, there were times when he just had to get away; he would disappear for days, weeks. I always knew he was safe. It was just what he needed. Molly said that he was thinking. I don't doubt that. He will be hunting, climbing and thinking. He will be trying to find as many ways as possible that he can touch you and you won't change. Although thinking of my son that way is a bit yucky." Jane screwed up her nose. Selene couldn't help let out a small laugh. "That's the girl I know, with such a lovely smile. You have to have hope. If you don't have that, you have nothing."

"Was it easy living with a shifter?"

"Apart from the fur balls and the spraying all over the furniture, it was good. Seriously, have a broom handy for when they do the marking thing. A quick swipe and they soon leave with a growl."

"I did notice a lot of rubbing on the furniture when I was in Montana." She perked up.

"Did you see the big scratching post that they had as well?"

"I did. I admit they had to explain it to me first. I didn't really believe what they were saying. I had a go, though. Shifted my hands and had a good scratch. It was actually very therapeutic."

Jane leaned forward and looked around. Kas was at the counter eating a burger specially prepared for him. They both knew the bear had super hearing and would be listening in to every word they said. "I had a go as well. Broke a bloody nail, but it was so worth it."

They both laughed. When Kas chuckled, Selene had the proof she needed that he was using his abilities. In a matter of minutes, Jane had turned Selene's mood around. She wasn't sure how her surrogate mother had done it, but her heart and head felt lighter.

"You have to remember with Brayden, as I had to with Heath, it will never just be the two of you. They are part of a pack, blood, though not defined by DNA, brought together by a need for companionship. That was the thing I found the hardest at the start. When you marry, you think, ok, I'll be living alone with this man, but I wasn't. I was living with him and a whole lot of others. I didn't even give birth to Brayden in a hospital. It was in the room that is now his at the house, surrounded by the females of the pack, each of them helping out. I was terrified but felt so at home at the same time. I'll never forget the roars and barks of celebration when I safely delivered and recovered from the complications."

"Is that why you came here when Heath died? Surely you could have stayed with the pack." It was a question of genuine interest to Selene. In the short time, she'd been with the pack she'd felt loved and wanted.

"I could have, they didn't want me to leave. A part of me didn't want to go either, but I needed something for myself. Brayden was old enough to live with Kas. I knew he would be protected and cared for. That was his home. He was already outgrowing the need for his mother. That is a male cat's way. I shut my eyes and stuck a pin in a map of America, and it landed in Death Valley. It could have been anywhere. Even down the road from Glacial Park but fate gave me here. Of course, I told Brayden that it was because I wanted some sunshine, so he didn't think it was as random as it was. I like it here, though, and I know that if I need my family, they will be there for me."

"Would you ever move back?"

Jane looked over to Kas, the bear's eyes shut.

"I don't know. That is my honest answer. When you and Brayden have children, because it is a when not an if, I want to be near them, but I'm not sure if I want to live in a house full of people anymore. I like my independence now."

"I'm sure Kas will let you open a little café in the park. Especially if you cook him seal burgers all the time."

There was that growl of a polar bear licking his lips at the thought again. She winked at him.

"Stop teasing him." Jane gave Kas a warm smile.

"I know, I'm sorry Kas." She spoke into the air but knew the message would be heard.

"Selene, all I'm trying to say is: at the moment things look bad, but it will work out. I have been in a dark place. The days after Heath died I thought that my life was over, but I found my strength. Everything happens for a reason. Isn't that what you believe?"

"I was put here for a reason and I exist because I was created."

"You exist because you were given to those that need help." Jane's words resonated through her. "I should go check on the kitchen. Do you think you can eat now?"

"I do. I'm going to eat and then go back to Montana. Brayden and I need to talk."

"Good girl. Give him a big hug from his mother and yours." Jane smiled.

"You know I will."

She took another bite of the burger, and it tasted good. Suddenly the world didn't feel like too bad a place. They would find a way.

"Well, look who decided to come back. Have you been off practicing your prick teasing elsewhere?" A voice that she had hoped never to hear again interrupted her meal.

"Stuart. I would say I've missed you, but I would be lying. How are the balls? Swelling gone down yet?"

"I warned you that you would pay for that." He sneered callously.

"Yes, you did. Maybe we should take this outside. I would hate for you to be embarrassed in front of your friends." Their voices were quiet so nobody would hear them. All except Kas--he rolled his eyes. He knew what she would be doing next.

She pushed the table out to get up. It was only a subtle boost, but she stopped it just before it hit Stuart on the other side. She smiled sweetly and then slammed the table directly into his legs. He yelled out in pain such was her force. She liked this new-found strength thing and was glad the spell hadn't affected that. Although she did secretly wish she could hear Stuart's thoughts right now.

"Bitch." He jumped over the table and went to pull her hair, but she was quick enough to sidestep him, catch him by the arm, and rammed him headfirst into the booth. She heard his nose crack, and blood splattered everywhere.

"I hope daddy can afford another nose for you," she quipped snidely.

He lifted his head quickly and went to slam it into hers. She was able to move at the last minute, but he caught her shoulder which sent pain through it. That was quickly shaken off when Stuart came for her again and punched her in the face. Pain crashed through her body, and she was grateful she'd become so accustomed to getting hit by Emma that it didn't knock her out. She sensed Kas behind her.

"No." She held her hand up. "This fight is mine."

"Who the fuck is he?" Stuart looked up at Kas.

"Someone who is welcome here, unlike you." Jane stepped forward. "How dare you come into my restaurant and hit a woman."

"She hit me first. Everyone saw."

He lunged at her again, but she twisted her body so that she was able to kick out and send him flying to the floor in a heap. He was dazed and tried to stand but couldn't. She put the heel of her boot into the arch of his back and applied a little pressure. He screamed.

"A month ago, I went on a date with this man." The restaurant was full, and people from outside must have heard the commotion because they were appearing at the door. "He took me to a lookout point and tried to have his way with me. I said no. That's when he tried to rape me. Thankfully, Mrs Dillon's son was around to rescue me." She pushed her foot down harder. She looked around at some of the girls in the room, who'd gone pale. "I suspect that I'm not the only one that he's forced into giving up a part of themselves to feed his over-inflated ego." One of the girls stood up.

"He made me give him my virginity, he said he loved me but never spoke to me again." A young blonde stood and stepped forward.

"He did the same to my sister, got her pregnant as well. His Daddy forced her to have an abortion." An angry looking brunette called out from the back of restaurant.

"He beat me black and blue when I wouldn't suck his dick. I've still got scars." The final girl pushed her way through the crowd and lifted up her top to show a two-inch scar on her stomach.

"Miss Harper, I should be asking you to let go of Mr Henderson and arresting you for assault," The sheriff said as he appeared at the door. Kas was right by Selene's side, he would get her out of there if need be. "But, I think I must have got something in my eyes because I didn't witness any assault. Mr. Henderson had a funny turn after hearing his many wrongdoings finally being exposed. He stumbled against a table, a booth and the floor; I'm sure everyone in here saw that. Jessie? Caroline? Bethany?" The three girls who had spoken up stepped forward. "I think we need to take statements from you three, and anyone else that has a story to tell about Mr. Henderson. Deputy." A scrawny little man appeared. "Take the girls to my office and interview them, please. I'll bring Mr. Henderson in."

Selene pushed her foot one final time into Stuart's back causing him to cry out again. The sheriff smirked. "Miss Harper, I want to thank you for making a citizen's arrest. I hope to see you around town a lot more."

"Thank you, Sheriff."

The sheriff took Stuart from under her boot and pulled him out the door. The crowd in the restaurant approached her one by one to give her thanks before dispersing. Kas pulled down the strap of her cardigan.

"Excuse me?"

"Cream." He pulled a tube of the lotion that Brayden rubbed on her bruises previously.

"Seriously, you carry that stuff around with you?" she huffed.

"Always. I've learnt to expect the unexpected. Even more so since you arrived," Kas grumbled.

Jane came up to her and gave her a massive embrace.

"Oh my God, you were so brave. Nobody has ever stood up to him. I know his father is going to be livid out at this. Maybe the town will realize now they don't need to back down to him all the time."

"I hope so. Maybe we should stay here a little while longer to ensure everything is alright?" Selene suggested.

"I'll be fine," Jane quickly replied.

"I have allies nearby. I will have them come here immediately to keep watch." Kas pulled his phone out of his pocket and started to dial.

"Kas, there is no need." Jane frowned.

"No arguments." Selene shook her head at Jane, there was no point in trying to argue with him

"Stuart's father will be spending the next few hours trying to get his son out of jail. The people of this town have hated that family for a long time. You've brought about change. See? I told you; you exist because you were given to those that need help." Jane was so happy with her.

"I guess." Selene felt a sense of pride

"You better believe it. Now go find my son."

CHAPTER THIRTEEN

"Welcome back Selene." Scott sidled up to her and put his arm around her shoulders. "It's good to see your happy, smiling face back in our home. Can I help you to your room with your bags? Or rather, get Tyler to carry them to your room?"

"Hey, what?" The wolf looked confused.

"I'm alright Scott, my bag is light. I think I can manage it." Selene smiled sweetly and shrugged off Scott's arm.

"Yeah, back off, the lady needs room to breathe and not have your stinky lion breath all over her the second she walks in the door." Katia greeted her with a kiss on the cheek.

"Bloody male chauvinist pig. Sorry, lion." Emma kissed the other cheek. "She doesn't want you in her pants, remember the conversation we had where I said you are not God's gift to women. You're a big pain in the arse, and your mane is going gray."

"You lie!" It was the lion's turn to look shocked. "How could you say something like that? I'm not turning gray. Selene, please, she's lying, isn't she?" Before she had time to answer Scott was running up the stairs with his hands in his hair.

"That was mean, Emma, he'll be in front of the mirror all day now checking for gray hair," Kas grumbled.

"Yes, but we will get some peace and quiet." Emma gave an evil cackle.

"Here." Zain stepped forward and handed her a plate. "It's a honey sandwich to say sorry for making you so upset you had to leave. I know I get a bit protective of my honey, but I do so like it."

"Um. Thank-you." She looked at the dripping mess on

the plate. It was more bread swimming in honey than a sandwich. I'll eat it later, if that is alright? I'd like to find Brayden first. Kas said you were probably the best person to take me."

"Of course. I'd like that. Miss Molly said he was up on Harrison's Glacier when she last saw him. We'll check there first." The bear was almost jumping with excitement.

"Emma," She handed her the plate. "Can you put that in the fridge for me for later, please?"

"You can't put honey in the refrigerator." Zain grabbed the plate back. "It goes all funny. No, I'll eat it to give me energy before we leave. I can make you a fresh one later."

"That's a good idea." Emma laughed behind Zain's back as the bear swallowed the sandwich in one gulp and then licked the plate.

"Let's go." Selene was ready, more than ready, to find her man.

It had taken them a while to get up the mountain; she wasn't as good a climber as the others. At one point Zain had transformed into a bear so that they could negotiate a rocky passage with ease. The further up they got the colder she felt. She could see why Brayden loved to be up here. His body temperature was definitely a degree or two higher than most other people.

If Death Valley felt like, well, death, then Glacial National Park was life. Even in the craggy rocky cliffs, plants grew, small alpines full of color. It was a heavenly place.

Zain got up on his hind legs, sniffed the air, and let out a roar. It was returned by a growl that she instantly recognized. It wasn't too far away. She started to run toward the sound, stopping when she realized Zain wasn't following.

"You're not coming?"

He shook his head and pointed to a river a little down the mountain.

"Salmon?"

He grunted.

"Is Brayden far?"

Zain motioned with his hand for her to go.

"Thank you."

Hopefully one day she would get the telepathic link that the others had so that she was able to talk to them in animal form. For now, she knew Zain was happy with finding his dinner. He was a bear, a simple bear, who thought primarily of his stomach and left more challenging things to the others.

She jumped over a small clearing and found herself in a lake of ice. It was beautiful. She'd never seen anything like it before, you didn't tend to get ice in Death Valley. She placed her hand down onto it. Cold. She pulled back and blew on her hand to warm it up. This was Brayden's home, his natural territory, his safe place. The rumbling mewl hit her before she saw him, in snow leopard form, appear from a shallow fault in the glacier. He was absolutely stunning. His sleek coat was splattered with black spots, his eyes were large and vibrantly green, and they stared into her very soul. He came before her, and she knelt in submission. He was a wild beast and deserved respect even though she knew he would never hurt her. She unbuttoned her shirt and folded it neatly beside her. Brayden's ears pricked up and he sat in front of her contentedly. She got to her feet, removed her jeans and knickers, and knelt back on the ice. Surely she should feel some cold, but she was surrounded by warmth that came from Brayden.

"I'm going to touch you," she cooed. He got to his feet and took a step back with a snort of disapproval. "Please. I know you don't want to hurt me. I accept what we cannot be for now. I give you whatever I can because I love you. I'm yours Brayden, in mind, spirit, and when we can, body. That will never change. I kneel on ice, but I feel no cold because you are with me. Let me be yours."

He stepped forward on large paws covered in white and black fur. Such was his magnificence and power that she knew that in one swipe, he could kill her. She felt so tiny in comparison to him. He lowered his head and with a slight quiver, she touched his soft fur. The tingle came instantly, and she started to shift, her entire body transforming itself. She shut her eyes as the last vestiges of her body switched. She knew when she opened them, the world would look different. How did a cat see? Was it in color? Brayden mewled; he was waiting for her.

She opened her eyes. Cats saw in color, but it wasn't as vivid. She had a wider vision but not as clear. It made her a little queasy. She inhaled a deep breath, and scents from all over engulfed her. A rustle nearby caught her now-enhanced hearing. She turned her head, her vision taking a moment to catch up. A bird hopped out of the bushes, took one look at them, and flew away. Brayden settled beside her and started to purr. His head nuzzled her side as he licked her fur.

Brayden got to his feet and mewled for her to follow him. He made sure to keep his tail touching her at all times. They jumped over a few rocks at a slow speed so that she could get used to being on four, not two legs. She found her stability and stamina before they chased through the park. They sprinted past Zain in the river. The big bear had a large salmon in his mouth and looked very happy. Eventually, they came to a stop before a cave. Brayden nodded for her to go in. It must have been the place he'd been sheltering since there were clothes and a blanket inside. She'd thought he would spend all his time as a leopard in the wild, but he must have changed a few times. She wanted to speak to him. She shut her eyes and thought hard on her words.

"Your home."

"Yes."

The word popped into her head. Her eyes sprang open, and she stared at him.

"You heard that?" The thoughts entered her head again.

"Yes." She concentrated on her reply.

"You are evolving with your powers. We will beat this one day."

"We will. But till then, I want this."

She was very careful to ensure that the tip of her tail still touched him but presented herself to him, her sex in animal form for him to take. He growled, the pupils in his eyes dilating. The cave had little light, but with her cat's eyes, she saw everything. They could not be mates in her natural form but in his, they could. They could join together as one and have a life. Brayden walked a circle around her, brushing up against her, marking her. He took her neck in his mouth, his teeth not breaking her skin, and she bowed to him. He was the master here.

She let out an impatient cry and was sure she got a chuckle in her head back, but her ability to form cognitive speech had disappeared. She had never wanted something so badly. Brayden mounted her back and she waited for him to enter her. Waited. Waited.

"I can't do it." He stepped away, human again, and she changed back to normal as well.

"Brayden. I want it. Please," she pleaded.

"I know you do. And I want so much to give you it because I want it too, but I want our first time to be special, not animalistic rutting."

She shivered, the cold suddenly getting to her.

"Cover me up in that blanket. We made progress today with the telepathy so it shows it can be done. We've got hope." Brayden picked up the blanket and pulled it around her shoulders. He made sure not to touch her flesh but held her as close as he could.

"I missed you."

"I missed you, too. Kas took me to see your mother."

"And she sent you straight back here."

"Sort of. But not before I dealt with Stuart. I did learn something from my lessons."

"You're turning into a formidable fighter." He smiled. "I spoke to Molly, the old puma I told you about once."

"I know, she told the others you ate all her dinner." She lightly punched him playfully in the stomach.

"I did not. I ate three-quarters of it." He pouted in response.

"You'll have to take me to meet her one day."

"One day?"

"When I can run on my own."

"You're not giving up?"

"No, I'll do this. I'll work it out. I'm going to ask Jessica to remove the spell so I can practice harder. I was created for a reason, and that is to be with you." She raised her hand to touch his cheek but stopped short of his skin.

"One day. One day we'll be together in every sense of the word."

"Why one day?" A crack of lightning flooded the cave, and Nuka appeared. Brayden stood in front of her; fangs displayed.

"Calm down pussy cat. I'm not here to harm you. I'm here to help you." Nuka rolled his eyes. "Cats. Pounce first, think later."

"Help? You've never helped anyone in your life." Brayden snarled.

"You've been painted an atrocious picture of me, haven't you? I bet Kas even told you I killed your father." Nuka crossed his hands over his chest to feign injury to his reputation.

"Kas said nothing, but I know that you were there."

"Yes, I was. I know what happened and all is not what it seems." Nuka barked back his teeth clenched.

"Are you trying to tell me Kas killed my father? Because I won't believe you."

"Alas, I have no proof of who killed your father, but I do have this." He pulled a phone from his pocket and pressed play. Kas and Jessica's voices appeared.

"Are you sure you can segregate the spell?"

"Yes, it's a simple adjustment. It won't take much."

"And she will not be able to touch Brayden without shifting?'"

"No. We'll control her. We can use her powers for our

needs."

"I will go and wake her, then."

She could feel it, through the blanket, every fiber in Brayden's body breaking down as he struggled to take in what was on the phone. It was a betrayal of the worst kind. Kas and Jessica had adjusted the spell so that she would not be able to touch him.

"I'm sorry that I had to be the one to bring that to you. I didn't want to, but I felt you needed to know. I also believe that may give you some insight into the murder of your father as well Brayden."

"They tricked us."

"Yes. And in the cruellest way. My brother craves power. Selene, you are a threat to that power. You have the strength to you to be what we cannot. An ultimate shifter—to be any animal, alive or dead—and that scares him because it means you are stronger than him."

"And he can never control me because the only person I will ever submit to is Brayden. My mate. We have the power to take over the pack." She could see that Kas' had misplaced fear in what she would do to the pack.

"I have a druid who can help you. He visited the Council shortly after Jessica and was given the spell as well. If you consent, we can go to him, and I'll have him perform the spell correctly. You can be together. I'll even allow you my master suite so you can consummate your relationship all day." He winked at them.

"How can we trust you?" Brayden was rightfully concerned, but he had an edge of hope in his voice.

"I lost everything with my grandfather's death. I've wanted revenge; I coveted it. I'm not afraid to say that. But what I want more than anything is for shifters to be free to live happily and not be governed by a Council that knows nothing about how we live. I want you two to have the freedom to live alone up here in the mountains if you wish. I don't think you should trust me; I want to give you something others don't."

"What do you think?" Brayden turned to her.

"I'm stunned that they betrayed us. I don't know who to trust. There's only you."

"Kas has always been controlling. He likes everyone in their place. I believe that he is scared the of the power you wield."

"But enough to keep you from finding happiness?"

"I don't know. Jessica seemed to enjoy the fact that your power amplified hers. She's always wanted to be a stronger sorceress."

"What about the others? Do you think they know?"

"I hope not. It will destroy the pack. I don't want to think about that. Right now we have to concentrate on what is best for us. If Jessica and Kas did indeed do this, we will demand justice later."

"Do you want to give the spell a try?" Selene asked him.

"We've got nothing left to lose." Brayden turned back to Nuka. "We will come with you."

CHAPTER FOURTEEN

Nuka's mansion was a palatial log cabin in the forest near Moraine Lake in Banff National Park. The snow leopard in him fought to explore, run free. He suppressed it for the more urgent need at hand.

"Thank you, Jackson." Nuka acknowledged the guy who had brought them some drinks. From the smell of him, he was definitely a feline. Probably a panther. Brayden tried not to growl at him.

"Ciaran will be here momentarily. He is finalizing what he needs for the spell."

"We've waited this long. We can wait a few moments more." Selene squeezed Brayden's hand as she spoke.

"I've asked one of the tigresses to prepare the room for after. You will be welcome here as long as you wish. I know I have a reputation of being a tyrant, but I hope that you'll find I'm not as bad as rumor paints me."

"We hope not as well." Why would Kas betray them like this? They just wanted to be an average couple. Was Selene really that much of a threat? Maybe Kas was not the man that Brayden thought he was. If so, then why had he cared for him like a son since his father had died? He was barely a man himself. Nothing made sense.

"How did you get the audio on your phone?" Something didn't add up to Brayden

"I wondered when you would ask. I have Kas' offices bugged."

"No, you don't. Jessica does regular sweeps."

"I'm afraid the witch's powers are inferior to those of my druid. After all, he was her teacher until she turned against him."

"Ciaran had an affair with a wild dog. I think she had a

right to turn against him." Brayden wasn't going to allow Nuka to paint Ciaran as a good man.

"She did not have the right to have him thrown off the Council. He was good at his job." Nuka barked back.

"That depends on your interpretation of the Council's rules. Jessica was his pupil, and the wild dog his subordinate."

"I see that we will not agree on this." Nuka stopped that particular with a wave of his hand. "I can assure you that the video came from one of my hidden devices." Brayden tried not to laugh. Nuka had the same attitude Kas had on occasions, even down to the pretentious tone.

"We will agree to disagree." He sat back and drank the coffee. Nuka's druid chose that moment to enter the room.

"Is everything ready?" Nuka asked.

"Yes. Please, Miss Harper if you would come this way. I've got everything set up in my room."

"I'm coming as well." Brayden stood and pulled Selene to her feet and to his side. She was not going anywhere without him.

"Of course, Brayden. We will not split you up." Nuka added.

The warlock led them through the cabin. It was tastefully decorated. Maybe a few too many stag horns for his liking but Brayden could guarantee they weren't fakes. They'd probably made a nice meal for everyone at some point.

"I know this is hard, but we need to give them a chance. Nuka didn't have to show us that video." Selene whispered into his ear. She was careful not to get too close.

"I'm being a moody snow leopard, aren't I?"

"Just a little." She wiggled her nose coyly.

"I'm just confused. And angry at being played for a fool by Kas."

"I know. I'm mad at him as well. I might try and change into that flea again and go bite him so many times that he gets really itchy."

"You're a little crazy at times."

"Makes me fun in amongst all the angst."

The druid held the door open to his room for them.

"Thank you." Selene strode in, her curvy backside swivelling in her tight jeans. Brayden caught Ciaran watching and growled.

"Sorry. It won't happen again."

"See that it doesn't."

He took a seat from the corner of the room and dragged it in one long scrape to where Ciaran pointed for Selene to stand.

"I'll need you to sit back a little please."

He growled again.

"Brayden, Selene is in safe hands. Please come sit near me. We will be safe from the spell here." Nuka had taken a seat on a comfortable sofa across the other side of the room. Brayden complied.

"The spell will be different from the one Jessica performed. I'm merely taking away the barrier she put in to prevent you from not shifting when you touch Brayden. Would you be able to hold these for me? They are a mixture of thyme, rosemary and ague weed. It is important you ball them in your hands. The touch element is important."

"This will not unbind all my abilities, will it?" Selene asked.

"No, it will simply allow you to touch Brayden and not shift. The spell Jessica put on you will still be in place. I cannot remove that, only she can."

"How do we know that it will work?"

"I'm afraid you have to trust me on that. I taught Jessica, my magic is stronger than hers. When I look at you I see a barrier, your aura is off. That is how I know what she has done and how to fit it."

Brayden watched Selene and Ciaran as they prepared for the spell. He drew magical symbols on her face in a paste made from apple. He'd asked Selene to stand in the middle of a pentagram. The white chalk of the magical mark was stark against the dark wooden floor. It reminded him of the fresh white of Selene's coat and the black flecks that marked it.

"She is brave." Nuka spoke up.

"Selene?"

"Yes. To not know anything about who she is but be able to maintain a sense of humor and strength is a powerful attribute." Nuka's voice was quiet and calm as he spoke.

"She has no past to be jaded by?" That was an unspoken truth between Brayden and Selene. He had a lot to show her and much of it would leave her upset. The world wasn't always a nice place.

"You speak again of your father?" Nuka inquired.

"My father, the Council's decisions to take the land. It has left many a shifter wanting to just disappear up into the mountains for a quiet life."

"You no longer want to fight?"

"I want to know if what I'm fighting for is worth it. They say humans are bad for the destruction they are raining down on the Earth, but we are no different. We say we live in peace, but you always hear of a brutal death, another displaced animal. It happens so minimally compared to the fights of the past, but it still happens. We all strive for dominance in this world. Maybe we are just animals in the end. Humanity died years ago." There was such despondency in his answer.

"You are a bright man Brayden; I could do with a man like you in my pack. You see things, the subtle occurrences that other shifters miss. You know something is coming, you sense it like I do."

"I'm a member of the Glacial Blood." His reply was curt.

"Even though they would betray you and the woman who is so obviously your mate?"

"Kas would have had a reason."

"Other than to destroy Selene's ability to take his power, I can't see what it is."

"And after I'm assured of Selene's safety, I will ask him."

Every muscle in his body tensed. He knew it. Nuka knew it. He would take Kas on in a fight to the death if it meant discovering the truth about why he prevented Selene from not shifting at his touch.

"Well if you ever want a position in my pack, know that it is yours."

"Thank you."

Ciaran commenced his spell. Selene knelt on the floor, the herbs balled in her hands, her head bowed as the druid recited his words.

'Devotio mala, devotio mala,
Upon mine safety, I doth hold,
Returneth the spell,
Back to whence it came,
Cleanse this vessel of thine hex,
That doth plague her pure blood,
Devotio mala, devotio mala.'

Selene put her head up. Her eyes had rolled back into her head. She was recanting the words in perfect time with Ciaran.

'Devotio mala, devotio mala,
Upon mine safety, I doth hold,
Returneth the spell,
Back to whence it came,
Cleanse this vessel of thine hex,
That doth plague her pure blood,
Devotio mala, devotio mala.'

The third time through, she thrust her head back and expelled a plume of black smoke. Her voice was a hoarse scream as it dissipated into the sky. He went to stand, but Nuka put his hand in the way.

"She is fine. It is the spell."

Selene collapsed, and Brayden was on the floor with her

in a second. She was gasping for air. He pulled her hair back from her face.

Her eyes focused on his hand. Touching her.

"I'm not changing." She was breathless. "It worked?"

"It worked."

"Thank you." She looked over to Nuka and Ciaran, her eyes full of gratitude. He had to admit he owed them a thank you as well but not before he'd had a taste of her lips. Their eyes met. She loved him. She was his mate.

He lowered his head to hers. Warm breath passed over his face when her breath hitched. He placed his lips desperately on hers and waited for the spell to fail, but it didn't. He could taste her; sweet honey mixed with rose. If anyone asked him again what his favorite taste was it would always be her. Even Molly's venison stew did not compare. His pulse quickened when she melted against him. He pulled reluctantly away.

He needed to get her into the nearest bedroom. "Where can we go?"

Nuka laughed.

"I thought that would be your first question. Ciaran, why don't you escort Miss Harper to the room we have prepared for them. I'm sure she could use a few moments to freshen up after the spell."

Selene's pupils were dilated, she swayed as if she was in a dream.

"That would be good. I think I need to lose some clothes." Selene winked at Brayden.

There was no way he would hold a growl in.

"Five minutes, and then you're mine."

He kissed her again, getting to his feet and pulling her with him. They parted, and she left the room with Ciaran.

"Thank you, Nuka. I know we've had our differences in the past. You didn't have to help us."

"She is special. I would not leave her unprotected as Kas did."

"Look, I'm not saying joining your pack is a no. I need to

confront Kas first. Will you give me time to think about it?"

"Of course. Take all the time you need. If you and Selene need anything while you are here, then just ask. I suspect though for the next few hours there will be little I can help you with."

"Yeah, I think I can handle everything for a while."

He held out his hand and shook Nuka's. "To new beginnings."

"Let me escort you to your mate."

"Thank you."

He followed Nuka through the cabin with a spring in his step.

"She's in here."

Nuka opened the door for him. "I'll have dinner put outside your door."

Brayden walked into the room and shut the door behind him. It was dark.

"Selene?"

Nothing. Had she fallen asleep?

The lights above him flicked on. He was in a cage. Shit. He saw the cage door in front of him and ran for it but was too late. It slammed magically shut.

"Selene?" Where was she? What was going on?

Another light turned on to reveal Selene in the middle of the room. She was bound and gagged; her arms hanging from the ceiling to keep her in place. Tears filled her eyes.

"Did you really think I would let my brother have such a precious commodity as his own?" Nuka stepped out of the shadows.

"I will fucking kill you." Brayden hollered out.

He rattled the bars of the cage. An electrical current surged through him and sent him flying backward. Selene screamed into the gag.

"I don't think so. I'll be the only one doing the killing. But not before Miss Harper gives me exactly what I want."

CHAPTER FIFTEEN

How could they have been so stupid as to trust Nuka? Kas had warned them, and they'd fallen straight into his twin brother's trap. Nuka didn't want them to be able to have a relationship. He wanted her and specifically her powers.

Her scream was deafening when Brayden flew through the air and landed in a heap on the floor of the cage.

"Leave him alone." Her words were barely distinguishable through the gag. Ciaran ripped it from her lips, and she spat at him.

"Play nice, Selene, or I'll stick you in the cage with Brayden. By the time we've finished with him, he'll be wilder animal than the man you know and love now."

"What do you want?"

"Selene, don't listen to them. Give them nothing." Brayden rushed forward again. This time he didn't touch the bars.

Nuka looked to Ciaran, who weaved his hands together and threw a ball of magical energy at Brayden. It hit him square in the chest, and he collapsed to the floor.

"Stop it. Just tell me what you want." She was desperate.

"Part of the spell that Jessica performed on you linked her to you. If you call her, she will release the spell." Nuka towered in front of her, his hands folded behind his back.

"I don't understand?"

"She will feel your emotions if you call for her. If you are desperate, then she will know it. If you need your powers, she will release them. Call her."

"No." Brayden, trying to stand, called again, and Ciaran launched another energy ball at him.

"Stop that." She lashed out at Ciaran. "Why do you want

my powers released? I'm not going to use them to help you. I don't even have control over them."

"No, you can't. And that is perfect for us." Ciaran slid forward and laughed eerily. "Call Jessica, plead with your heart for your powers."

"Tell me why my not controlling them is better for you?" That answer had terrified her.

"Selene, you mustn't." Brayden was back on his feet again, his shirt burned away and the skin on his torso inflamed.

Ciaran balled another energy blast in his hands.

"You throw that at him, and I'll never call."

Nuka nodded at Ciaran. The Druid quashed the flame with a snarl.

"Spoil my fun, why don't you? Nuka, do you want to explain, or shall I?"

"You make the preparations. I'll explain to Miss Harper what is about to happen." Ciaran turned away and started to pull out potions from a box. "You will call for Jessica, Selene. I will make sure of that. I have ways. What you did not learn from my brother is that you are vulnerable until you learn control. Your powers can be ripped from your body and transferred to another. It will, of course, leave you dead."

"You want my ability to shift into anything?" Everything fell into place.

"I would be stronger than any member of the Council with your abilities and mine. I will take back my lands and destroy anyone that had a hand in my father and grandfather's death. You are a necessary sacrifice."

"I will not call her," she replied adamantly.

"Ciaran." Nuka stepped back so she could see the cage. Brayden's feet rose into the air. His arms flung out. He was being stretched. An agonized growl left his body before he fell to the floor. He looked up at her. His eyes were dark with fury.

"Don't give him what he wants," he spat out venomously.

"I can't watch him hurt you." It was too painful. His body was breaking apart. Every cry was rooting itself deep inside her.

"I can withstand a lot more than this. Zain warns you about taking his honey. Well, I borrowed some once." His attempt at a reassuring laugh came out strained. "Let's just say I'm lucky I've still got arms and legs. I was in traction for a month."

"Brayden?"

He lifted off the floor again. This time, his tattered clothes ripped from his body leaving him naked. With a twist of his hand, Ciaran drew shallow cuts across his body, crimson blood marring his perfect pale flesh. She couldn't do this. She couldn't be strong.

"You can stop this, Selene. Make the pain go away for him. All you have to do is call Jessica." Ciaran yelled at her.

"I can't." She sobbed.

Ciaran flicked his hand, and more cuts appeared. Brayden's arms thrust out again, and his body stretched. Bones cracked. Ciaran released the spell, and he fell to the floor. An arm came out at a funny angle, he tried to get up but his strength was fading fast.

"Plead for your powers, Selene. Save the man you love."

She shut her eyes. If she couldn't see what was happening, then maybe it would go away. They would realize she would never give up. Brayden was asking her to be strong. She had to do it for him.

"Pull him out. He is weak enough not to attack now." Nuka gave Ciaran his orders.

"I'll still bind his arms. I don't trust him." She could hear the movement around her.

"Open your eyes, Selene. Look at your lover."

"Selene, whatever happens, know that I love you. Fight for who you are. Fight for your powers. Don't let them win."

Tears streamed down her cheeks. She opened her eyes.

Brayden was on his knees in front of her. He had burn marks on his torso, blood seeped from cuts all over his body, his arm was at a funny angle, and a knife was at his throat. Nuka held it there.

"One last chance, Selene. Call Jessica for your powers now, or I'll end his life."

This was it. She had to make a choice. Her life or Brayden's.

"I'm sorry." She looked at him. His eyes focused on her, and they were filled with love and sorrow. "I will always love you."

She screamed Jessica's name.

***

"Oh my God. That is delicious." Jessica took another bite of the spinach and ricotta lasagna. "Seriously, this is better than sex. Tyler, you have to try some."

Tyler, who'd cooked the meal, looked at her like she'd grown two heads, and sat down with his pork loin.

"It has green stuff in it. No meat."

"That's the whole point of vegetarianism."

"Emma, she is using that strange word again." Tyler popped a bite of pork in his mouth after calling out to the lioness who was sharpening her knives at the table.

"Jessica stop teasing the meat-eaters, remember you're outnumbered here. And Tyler, eat with your mouth shut."

"Hey." They both replied at the same time. Tyler with his mouth open and meat spitting out.

"I wasn't eating with my mouth open."

"And I wasn't teasing the meat-eater. I just happen to believe vegetables are better for you."

Tyler made a gagging noise.

"I may be alone now, but wait till Selene returns. She eats vegetables."

"If she's up the mountain with Brayden then she'll be getting raw meat." Scott strode in and served himself some pork. "Great feast man. You're the best cook. The women of this pack are useless."

"You want to rephrase that Scott?" Emma held up a knife.

Jessica tried to stay focused on the conversation, but a pain in her chest had her shifting uncomfortably in her chair. She placed her knife and fork down and took a sip of water. The discomfort spread.

"See, the veggies have made you ill already." Tyler finished off his pork.

The pain was getting worse. She placed her hand over her heart and let out an agonized groan.

"Jess." All three were at her side.

"What's wrong?" Tyler felt her forehead. "You've gone white as a sheet."

She pushed them away and stood up, but her legs couldn't hold her. The pain was getting worse; it was like her heart was breaking in two. Selene's voice hit her like a ton of bricks.

She was lifted and carried. The screaming in her head left it impossible to focus. Selene was in pain, so much pain. The spell. She needed to reverse the spell. Give Selene her powers back.

"Kas?" she managed to speak her leader's name.

"I'm here, talk to me. What is it?" Kas held her hand with great concern.

"We have to reverse the spell."

"Selene?"

"She's in trouble. Excruciating pain."

"Do it." There was no hesitation in Kas' voice.

She flipped the pages of the book to the right page. A quick read of the words reminded her of them. She thrust her head back and started to recite.

'Ease mine pounding heart right now,
Break the connection to thine vessel,
Freeth her from Magic once cast,

Giveth back abilities no longer bound.'

On the last word, she collapsed back onto the bed, gasping for air. The pain stopped, and the screaming in her head turned to silence.

"Did it work?" Kas stroked her head, his large hands calming her.

"Yes, but we need to find them fast."

"Do you any idea where they are?" Scott was there as well.

She shook her head.

"Don't worry. I do." Kas pulled his shirt over his head. "Nuka."

***

White illumination flashed through the room.

Selene's legs sagged, leaving her suspended by her bound arms. They hurt, but she barely registered it. All she could focus on was the knife at Brayden's throat.

"What happened?" Nuka asked.

"She has her powers back," Ciaran smirked. "Jessica never could stand to hear someone in pain."

"Check." Nuka flicked his head towards her.

The Druid obeyed, stepping up to her and placing his hand on her cheek. Markings started to appear on her skin.

"No," Brayden whispered. "I can't lose you. I've only just found you."

"We need to hurry. They will be searching for them now. Ciaran."

A ball of energy formed. This was the moment she would die. She prepared for peace, but the ball went straight into Brayden's head. His eyes closed and when Nuka let go of him, he fell to the floor.

"No. You said you wouldn't hurt him if I called!" she cried her plea.

Brayden wasn't moving. She couldn't even tell if he was breathing. He'd been hit in the head by that thing. His hair had burned away, and his skin smoked. He was supposed to be her savior. Oh God, Jane. Her son and husband lost. She should never have been created.

"Do it." Nuka stepped forward and removed his clothes. Ciaran was preparing the spell around her. A baby cried. A baby? Where did that come from?

'You will be the savior of the world. Destined for such great things. Mommy and Daddy will always love you. Be strong our child, have faith, know you are what is right. Know that his love will set you free.'

Brayden.

She had to get to him. Her vision shifted. It grew wider and darker, the colors less vivid. Then she fell onto all fours. Nuka and Ciaran feverishly cursed in the background. Fur-- snow leopard fur --was covering her body. She had turned, a predator ready to protect what was hers. The growl left her throat and echoed around the room. Her vision cleared, Nuka and Ciaran stood still in front of her.

"We've lost our chance." The Druid dropped a potion he was holding. "She can change independently.

"Then we ensure they are both dead."

That was not going to happen. She let out a fierce growl as she leaped at the man before he could become the thousand-pound killing machine that he was.

CHAPTER SIXTEEN

The brilliant white paw lashed out at her face, razor-edged claws lacerating the flesh on her shoulder. She let out a wail and thrust her own sharpened talons into Nuka's torso.

"You will pay for this. I will see you gutted from neck to navel and fed to the eagles in the park." She was deadly in her rage.

"You are confident for someone who has been a shifter for mere moments," Nuka pushed back into her head.

"You do not understand the power of love because nobody would be insane enough to even look your way."

Nuka knocked her back. Her four legs flattened to the floor, and she hit her head against the wall as she flew back. The pain didn't even register.

"You're weak because you are new. You do not have the power yet to beat me."

"You underestimate my strength, especially after what you just did to Brayden."

In a one-on-one fight with Nuka, she could not beat him. His bear strength was superior to that of a snow leopard. She could only change into something she'd touched. To plague him as a flea wouldn't buy her the time she needed. There was only one other animal that would be suitable. She shifted into a polar bear. As a male, Nuka still had strength on her, but the form gave her a better ability to fight. She ran for him, head-butting him in the face and causing him to stagger backward.

"I'm not the puny weakling you think me to be. I was created for a reason. That reason is to defeat people like you. Individuals who seek to destroy the shifters' way of life with greed."

"They killed my family. How can you say that is correct?"

"You grandfather killed to take what he did. That made him wrong. The Council lives to ensure justice."

"You are a fool, who knows nothing. You will see that soon." Nuka swung for her again. She deflected the blow.

"I know my own mind. Men seek to control and weaken through violence. You are no different. You are scared." Nuka lunged at her, but she stepped back. Ciaran was forming an energy ball in his hand. "You are afraid because I'm a woman who has more power than you can ever imagine." She quickly shifted into a witch and deflected Ciaran's energy ball into the wall. She formed her own and sent the druid flying into the cage. She shut the door with the power of her mind.

"I will deal with you when I've killed your Alpha." Vengeance ran through her blood.

Nuka struck from behind, his claws ripping through the muscles of her back. She yelled out in pain, but it would not deflect her need to tear down everything Nuka stood for. Jessica had not shown her much magic, but what she remembered, she used. At a wave of her hand, furniture flew around the room. The door opened and several of the other members of the Banff pack flooded in. A panther lunged at her, his jet black fur catching the edge of her vision, but a table slammed into him and rendered him incapable of further attack.

"Cease this, Selene. You can't win," Nuka called out in her head. "You're outnumbered."

A wolf dove at her leg and sank his teeth into her tender flesh. She shifted to a wolf of her own and returned the bite before turning back to a witch. Energy balls formed in her hands. With a twist of her them, the balls filled the room, smashing into the creatures who would attack her. She was beyond reason, a dead woman walking, but she would take as many of them out with her as possible.

It happened in an instant, she was frozen in mid-air, the

wind sucked out of her in a long breath as she tried to free herself with the power of her mind.

"Thank you, Ciaran." Nuka shifted to human.

The druid held her in a spell. She glared down at him through the metallic bars of the cage.

"They will come for you. They will destroy you. Your brother may have had doubts in the past, but with this betrayal, he will seek your death." Her voice was feral. Nothing of the innocent Selene was left. She had become a wild animal. Her head turned in an almost eerie manner to the floor where Brayden still lay. "Did you kill his father, Nuka?"

"You are about to die, and that is what you want to know?" Nuka laughed demonically.

"Did you kill his father?"

"No." The answer was defiant. "Ciaran. Kill her."

The druid prepared his energy balls, and she shut her eyes for the second time today to prepare for death. This time, it would be sweet. She would join Brayden.

The blast of white light blinded her.

The light cleared, and she was still in Nuka's dungeon. But this time she wasn't alone. Jessica, Kas, Tyler, Scott, Emma, Zain, and Katia were there, ready to fight. Jessica made short work of freeing her from the magical chains while Kas went straight for his brother.

"Brayden. We need to get him out of here." Jessica was one step ahead of her and already at his side. She watched as the witch reached out to put her hand on the pulse in his neck.

"He's alive, but barely." He was still alive. She could barely breathe. "Selene, I need you to stay and help the others. I'm going to transport him to Molly's."

"I'm not leaving him."

Brayden groaned when Jessica wrapped her arms around him.

"Be brave. He would want you to protect his family."

"Family?"

"That is what we are. We have nobody else but each other." The words were spoken by the witch with love.

Everything fell into place, why Brayden had referred to them as his family even though he had Jane, why he stayed with people to whom he had blood-tie. They'd all fought against some atrocity in the past, and it had come down to this. They had each other, and they would protect that to the death. She would do the same. They were her family as well.

"You never put a spell on me to prevent Brayden and I being together?"

"What are you talking about?"

"Nothing. Your answer gives me all I need. Take him." Selene turned, and as the flash of white cascaded around her, she re-joined the fight.

***

"What did you think you would accomplish with this?" Kas deflected a strike from his brother.

"Revenge, brother." Nuka stumbled back as Kas rammed his fist into his brother's face.

"I brought peace to our family. The Council would have taken everything if we'd chosen to fight."

"Together we could have been strong. We could have defeated them."

"Defeat the Council? Are you insane?"

They were fighting in human form, while all around them others fought in animal form. He stepped forward and went for his brother's face again, white fur growing on his fist when he did so. In polar bear form, they would fill the room, eight feet tall on hind legs and pure muscle. He needed to put Nuka in his place, and this was the only way to do it. The roar of dominance that left his sharp-toothed jaw caused the room to shake. Nuka responded in kind, also now in polar bear form. The fighting around them stopped, the other shifters seeming to sense that this was Kas and

Nuka's duel.

"I gave you your own pack to rule." They circled each other. Their massive paws, laden with sharp, blood-covered claws, hammered on the ground.

Nuka growled.

"You have tried to take the lives of two members of my pack."

"Selene is not a part of your pack yet," his brother retorted.

"She is protected by the member of my pack that you tried to kill. That makes her part of our pack."

"Come now brother, what would you use her powers for? To help you and the witch control everyone to your whim?"

"I would use her for the reason she has been created."

"Nobody knows why she was created."

"She is here to help people. As all shifters of her kind are."

Nuka laughed.

"You actually believe that? She is dangerous. No multi-shifter has ever been female. Purposely not created so that they cannot breed."

"You think she was given to me to create an army of multi shifters?"

"I don't believe that she was given to you for anything. You may have stopped me from taking her powers away, but I still have her body."

The pack closed tighter around Selene.

"I will be no one's breeding vessel, she spoke out.

"I see now that I should not have allowed you to branch out on your own, brother. You were never meant to rule. That was my destiny as the elder brother; not yours. As a child, you were not taught the humility you need for the position. The power I gave you has gone to your head, and I must take it back. Effective immediately the Banff and Glacial packs are merged together. I'm removing you from your position as leader. Your pack will answer to my rule."

Nuka lunged at him, his paws flying, teeth snapping. His brother caught his shoulder and pain ripped through it. It was not enough to defeat him, though. He, too, was on his hind legs, his powerful legs, matching his brother punch for punch, his fangs ready to tear through flesh.

Nuka had appeared to be on his back foot, but now he stood taller and caught Kas off balance. The swipe to his face sent him tumbling backward, and Nuka was on him, his jaws wide and ready to bite down.

One of the disadvantages of being the weight of two Harley Davidson XL Sporters was if you went down; it wasn't that easy to get back up again.

He used his back legs to kick out at Nuka's chest. Nuka lost his balance this time, and they both rolled on the floor with teeth bared. Kas bit down on Nuka's left paw, which reopened the wound on his shoulder.

"Brother, stop this now."

"Never. You betrayed our family. You sold out our revenge for our grandfather's and father's deaths. I'll never rest until you are dead and I rule."

"The Council will never allow you to rule."

"Then I'll kill the fucking Council. I'll kill all the humans on this plain as well, if I have to. What is rightfully our family's was taken away from us, and I will not rest until I have it all back."

"You will die first."

"So be it."

Kas summoned the last of his strength to get the upper hand. He pushed Nuka to the floor and wrapped his teeth around his brother's jaw. One bite and he would kill him. The pack would be safe. He was the leader, he had to do it. He had to protect the Glacial Blood. Nuka was no longer his family. He started to bite down

A shaft of energy sent him flying back. Another flashed past from his pack. Ciaran had prevented him from killing Nuka.

He would have done it. He would have killed his own

brother. Nuka's pack stepped forward and pulled him back into their folds. His pack did the same to him. A standoff ensued.

"Do we finish this, Kas?" Emma was primed and ready for the fight.

Kas shifted back to human, his body bruised and bloody. "Nuka, will you stand down?"

"Never." His brother had shifted as well and was rubbing at his neck.

"Then the war begins." "Jessica?"
The flash of white light appeared, his pack held hands, and they were transported home.

CHAPTER SEVENTEEN

"How are you feeling? Do you need more balm?"

Kas shook his head as Jessica walked into his office.

"I think most of the wounds have nearly healed. How is Brayden?"

"Still sleeping. Selene is with him. She's refused to leave his side." Kas was glad that Selene and Brayden had each other and finally found the ability to be a couple.

"I don't blame her. They are mates. She is probably very scared. Did she say anything about how Nuka trapped them?" He asked.

"Apparently he showed them a video of us talking about binding Selene's powers but not against Brayden."

"What? We never discussed that." He slammed his fist on the desk. "How did he manage that."

"I don't know. Magic? Computers? A bit of both? I'm just as confused as you are. Apparently, he claimed he had this office bugged."

"But you check for that."

"I do, but maybe Ciaran is more powerful than I am." Jessica looked disheartened. Ciaran had betrayed her in the worse possible way and this had dented the witch's confidence.

"I don't believe that for a second. When Selene is healed maybe, both of you can go over the office together. Combine your magic."

"We won't have to wait for that. She has fully healed already."

"What?"

"It seems that Selene heals even quicker than we do."

"We really need to find out more about her." He motioned for Jessica to sit while he opened a drawer and pulled out a bottle of single malt whiskey. "I think we both need and deserve this." He poured two glasses and slid one across the table to her. Jessica had her roots in Scotland. She no longer had the brogue of a true Scot, but she could national drink like a true caber flinging, kilt wearing Highlander.

"We do." She took a draught. "I've arranged for Selene and Brayden to meet a multi-shifter from the Council. I'm hoping he'll shed more light on Selene's abilities. I fear that she is unique, even among her kind. I don't know why she was given to us, but we need to protect her. I was thinking we should get Jane back here. Brayden will want his mother protected."

"I will send for Jane tomorrow. I'm sure she will want to see Brayden when she learns of his injuries." He finished his glass and poured another.

"What are you going to do about Nuka?" Her question was hesitant.

"I wondered when you would ask."

"You were going to kill him, Kas. I've known you long enough now to know how that would affect you."

"He ceased to be my brother a long time ago. Unfortunately, I didn't realize that until today." It hurt him to admit that. He'd always hoped that Nuka could be brought to heel.

"Have you reported him to the Council?"

"I have. They will send someone to investigate. I doubt they will even get on Nuka's lands though. My brother will have a price on his head, be captured and neutralized."

"I'm sorry."

"Don't be. You and the others are my family now, and you're the ones who must be protected."

A loud crash came from the kitchen.

"What now?" Kas groaned wearily.

"Scott and Emma went out hunting. There was talk of needing something at least the size of a stag for dinner."

"I can't argue with that. As long as it is covered in seal blubber."

"I think Tyler was getting some out of the freezer when I left."

"Good." Kas stood and held his hand out for her. "Why don't you go see if you can find something without a pulse for you to eat?"

"Are you going to join us?"

"Soon." She left the room, and he sat back at his desk. He needed to make another call he'd been dreading. When he picked up the phone his hand was shaking. He found the number and pressed the call button.

Jane answered on the first ring.

"It's Kas."

"Brayden?" He could hear the alarm in her voice.

"He was in a fight. He's banged up pretty bad, but he is recovering. Selene is with him."

"What happened?"

"Nuka."

"Oh."

"It's started, Jane. What we always feared has begun. I need you to come here for protection. I'll send one of the pack."

"Can you give me a few days to sort everything?"

"Of course. I would come to get you myself, but..."

"It's ok, I know you're busy."

"Brayden was alone with Nuka for quite a while. I've not been able to speak to him yet."

"Do you think he knows?"

"Selene hasn't said anything. She was there all the time as well."

"He can't ever know what happened to Heath. Please, Kas."

"I know. Just sort everything out and come here to safety." He could hear her crying at the other end of the phone. He wanted to comfort her.

"I will. Goodbye."

"Goodbye, be careful."

"I will."

The line went dead. He placed his phone back down on the desk. There was still a small mouthful of the scotch in his glass. He picked it up, got to his feet, and he was faced with the picture of him and Nuka on his wall. Hatred burned through his veins. It was never supposed to be this way. He had made a life for his brother, and it was all being thrown back in his face. The only way it would end would be with his brother's death. He threw the glass at the picture. The scotch splattered over the happy, smiling faces of the cubs.

"I have no brother."

***

His head hurt like he'd drunk a whole keg of whiskey and then added another one just to make sure he was drunk. That sort of pain must mean he wasn't dead, only injured. He prayed for quick healing. One eye slowly opened. The room was dimly lit, but he was definitely in his own bed.

"Brayden." Selene's voice echoed from across the room.

"Selene." He tried to sit up.

"No. Don't move. Just rest. I'll get you some water."

"How did we escape?"

"The others came for us."

"How did they get there so quickly?"

"Oh, they didn't." She helped him to sit up a little. "Take a drink and lay back down again."

"Then how did they not kill you? Or are you a ghost? Nobody told me injuries would still hurt in the afterlife."

She laughed.

"I can assure you that you are very much alive, and so am I. I got control of my powers." She held her hand up and shifted it to a wolf's paw, lion's, tiger's, polar bear's, then witches' markings, and finally, she shifted into a snow leopard. The last one she let linger a little longer. "That one is definitely my favorite."

"How did you get control, just like that?"

"It was a very stressful time, and it seems my inner shifter did not like the man who would hurt her mate. When they hit you in the head, all I could think about was getting to your side. Shifting into a snow leopard gave me the ability to do that."

He needed something stronger than water. "We can be together?"

She smiled, a great, beaming one that told him what she was thinking. The smile vanished.

"Although, not until you're healed."

"Good job I heal fast, then," he purred, and she rolled her eyes.

"Male felines, you think only with one part of your anatomy. I'll go get you some food. Scott went hunting."

"Damn, why didn't I wake sooner. I would have loved to have seen that. But no, I'm not hungry, I'm tired again. Will you just come and let me hold you?"

"No funny business."

"I promise to be at peak physical capacity the first time I mark you."

"Sounds so romantic." He held back the sheets so she could climb into the bed. His arm went around her, and she nestled against his chest. She was touching his skin. He was touching hers. She wasn't changing.

"Brayden?"

"Yes."

"When you were unconscious, I asked Nuka something."

"What?" He kissed the top of her head.

"I asked if he was the one who killed your father."

He tensed.

"What did he say?"

"He said he didn't."

"Did you believe him?"

She swallowed. He felt it against his chest.

"Yes, I did."

If Nuka didn't kill his father, then who did?

CHAPTER EIGHTEEN

She woke up to warmth wrapped around her. Skin touching her skin. She and Brayden had spent their first night together in each other's arms. She could see his breathing was still shallow. He was still sleeping, and the last thing she wanted to do was wake him. Trying her hardest to get out of the bed, a calloused hand caught her arm and pulled her up against a rock-hard body.

"Where do you think you're going?"

"I was going to get you a drink and look at changing the bandages when you woke."

He put his head up and shook like a cat drying itself. The bandages came off and revealed a perfectly healed face. Even his hair was back at its former long length.

"Or maybe just remove the bandages?"

He growled and pressed against her. She felt his very hard and very large erection. It was time.

"I will take it slow for you, but I need to know now. If you have any doubts about being my mate, you must speak now, or it will be too late."

Doubts? Did she have any? She'd been created for good, she knew that, but she also happened to think that she'd been designed for Brayden. He would fit her perfectly and vice versa.

"No doubts." Her answer may have sounded a little more desperate than she had planned.

He flipped her onto her back and rose before her.

"I'm sick of having something between us. The clothes need to go. You are not to wear any again until I say you can." He pulled her T-shirt over her head and began to shuffle her bottoms down her legs. He inhaled a long breath when his head was level with her hips and his eyes focused on her sex.

"Wet already, I like it."

She wasn't just wet but dripping. She needed him inside her.

"Brayden, please?"

He chuckled. "Desperate?"

She couldn't lie. "Extremely."

"I've no intention of just a quick fumble. I've wanted my mouth on your flesh for so long, I'm going to savor every second."

He brought his lips down on hers, tenderly at first, but then his tongue demanded admittance to her mouth. She was lost to the passionate exchange of tongues twisting and searching. He pulled away, and she sighed dejectedly, but that turned into a groan when he wrapped his talented lips around one of her peaked nipples. In her mind, her creator had seen fit to give her perfect breasts, not too big and not too small. Just what she needed and oh, oh, oh...so, so sensitive nipples. He grazed his teeth over the right one while twisting the left. She arched her back off the bed.

"Fuck." Selene was close to orgasm already. Brayden purred his satisfaction and ground his hips into her thigh. He moved his mouth lower down her body, his teeth nipping into her flesh. Each touch was like an earthquake pulsating through her body. Only Brayden could make her feel this way. He parted her legs and licked up her thighs, interspersing it with bites. He hovered above where she really needed him to touch her the most.

"I'm going to wear this scent for the rest of my life. Not only will you be marked as mine, I'll be marked as yours."

"Always."

He parted the petals of her sex with his hands and drove his tongue through her slit to her clitoris. She was almost off the bed again, her hands shifting to paws so she could grip the sheets. He lapped up her juices, mewling contentment as he went.

She could barely breathe. Her whole body felt like it was

on fire. She undulated in need, burning for the explosion she knew would come.

"Brayden." She could barely talk. "More."

He twisted his fingers inside her to a soft spot that made her even less able to control herself.

"Come for me, Selene. Only for me." He bit down on her clit and pressed his fingers against the tender spot inside her.

She came apart. She called out his name, shaking and quaking like she was a bundle of euphoric nerve endings. She couldn't focus. She couldn't even open her eyes. The sheets were ripped to shreds, but all she cared about was the orgasm she was riding. What seemed like hours later, she came down; gasping for breath with aftershocks causing tremors in her legs.

"You are the most amazing sight when you come." Brayden removed his fingers from inside her and brought them to her lips to taste.

"I want to taste you."

He gave a shit-eating grin.

"I was hoping you would say that." Brayden lay back on the bed.

She hesitantly took hold of his cock. He was already so hard beneath the skin of her hand. She struggled to fit her hand around the full girth. He curved bigger in the center of his shaft before tapering down to the tip. The head was purple and looked like it was pulsating. Brayden placed his hands over hers and helped her establish a rhythm with her stroke.

"The touch of snow," she whispered.

His hands left hers, and he placed them behind his head. She could wait no longer to taste him. Bending over, she allowed her tongue to flick over the tip. Then she licked him again. This time down the length and back up. His penis was sensitive. Shifting her tongue to that of a cat she licked. He groaned out a long rumbling response.

"Holy shit."

She pushed him into her mouth in the next movement. He was so big.

She alternated licks around his shaft with circling her lips up and down it. Every now and then she would flick the head of his cock.

"Teach me more."

"Use one of your hands on my balls. Caress them. They are particularly sensitive so don't squeeze too hard."

She cupped the jewels within her hand and massaged them. She wondered what they tasted like, and realized when Brayden hissed that he'd heard her thought. She laughed around his cock, the reverberations seeming to make him swell within her mouth. She let him out with a pop and sucked on one of the balls while stroking his length. Her grip was hard and twisting.

"Babe. I'm going to come. You have to stop."

"I want to taste you."

"Do you not want me inside you? I don't know if I can do both, not with the healing."

She let go of him.

"Well then. I choose to have you inside me. We've got plenty of time for a gourmet tasting session later. We've got a whole lifetime for that."

"You're not fertile at the moment. Do you want to go without a condom?"

"How do you know?" She asked.

"Male cats are primed to tell. I've got condoms in the drawer."

"What about diseases and things like that?"

"I'm clean. I know you are clean."

"Then I want to be with you skin on skin. We've had enough barriers to touching in our life already."

Brayden moved over her and settled between her parted thighs. She felt him at her entrance and then the pressure of his penis pushing in. She tried to relax, but he filled her so fully. She felt a snap of temporary pain indicating she was no longer a virgin. She'd given a precious gift to her mate.

"Am I hurting you?"

She wasn't in pain, she just felt full and happy. He changed his angle, and his cock slid against her engorged clit. That was all it took. She climaxed again. Her body shook around his dick. When she looked at Brayden his fangs had appeared, and he was biting down on his lip.

"Sorry," she captured her breath and spoke.

"Don't ever apologize for taking pleasure." He snarled at her. "This mating works both ways, Selene. You will forever me mine and I'll forever be yours, as well. You want my body to get you off. You take it. I'll never say no."

He pulled his hips back and thrust back in. She gasped out loud. "Can you come again for me?"

Fucking yeah she could. She could come all day and all night. She might not walk again but hey, who needed to move around? She could fly, anyway. She was already doing that with Brayden inside her.

She rotated her hips to give Brayden his answer. He pulled her legs around his body and took her animalistic thrusts. Her hands wrapped around his thick, corded neck. She needed him closer. She needed him so deep inside her that he would never leave; she would forever feel him there. Her nails changed to jet black talons and embedded themselves with the taught flesh of his back.

His cock was hitting that special place inside her. She was going to come again. She could barely focus. She couldn't breathe.

"Selene, will you be my mate?"

"Yes. Yes." She came again, floating on a cloud of pure bliss. Brayden bit down on her shoulder, marking her. His mate. His. She flew even higher. His name left her mouth in a powerful roar. That set Brayden off, and he released within her, flooding her with his scent. Another mark that she was his.

Slowly they recovered. Her shoulder ached, but it was a pleasant ache. It was one that labelled her as finally part of a family. Finally, she was something, someone who belonged.

A knock came to the door. "Jessica wondered if Selene needs cream for the marking?"

"Fuck off Tyler." Brayden roared

There was another snigger outside the door.

"And you Scott," she added.

"Seriously. Kas says to get your arse's downstairs for breakfast, or he'll come up and get you. We've got to do the whole welcoming Selene to the family thing."

"We'll be down soon." Brayden pulled her into his arms and grinned. "Just as soon as I've done that all over again. We've got lost time to make up for."

CHAPTER NINETEEN

"Deeper baby. Deeper. Take more down your throat." Brayden had his hand wrapped around Selene's hair, and she was sucking him off in the seat of his Mustang in the middle of Death Valley. "Oh yes. Oh God. I'm going to come. You still want to taste me?"

"You try to pull my head away, and I'm releasing my fangs."

He pushed his head back against the seat and allowed himself to relax. Selene took him deep, and he couldn't hold back any longer. His balls drew up, and he released himself down her throat. She took every last drop of him before licking him clean.

He watched her while she reapplied her lipstick. She was exquisite in his eyes. His vision of beauty. His mate.

"What time is he due?"

"Anytime now."

They were back in Death Valley, a week after their mating, to meet the only other multi-shifter that would talk to her. Ethern Lennox. He'd insisted on having the meeting here, which didn't appeal to Brayden.

"We better get out."

"Do we have to?" The second he got out of the car, he would be melting again.

Selene opened her bag and pulled out a little fan. "Here. It's the best I can do, I'm afraid. At least it will keep you cool until we can get you back in the car."

"You're the greatest mate ever."

"I know."

The heat hit him the second he opened the door.

"Once this meeting is done, we're never coming back to this place. If you want a holiday, we're going to Antarctica.

No arguments."

"I thought we could go see where your family originate from in India when we have time."

"That... I might consider."

He stood behind her, his hands around her waist.

"Already?"

"I can't help it. You're in heat. Blame the snow leopard, not me."

"Your relationship seems to be solidified already. It's good to see." A man in a dark cloak appeared before them.

"Selene, Brayden. I'm Ethern. It is a pleasure to meet you." The posh-spoken Brit held his hand out. Selene shook it without hesitance, but he held back.

"Brayden?" Selene questioned.

"Have you changed to a snow leopard before?"

"I have. Do not worry. I'll not be collecting your power today. I'm merely being polite."

Brayden reached out and shook his hand.

"It's good to meet you as well. What can you tell us about Selene?"

"Straight to business. No small talk first?"

"It's over hundred degrees out here. I'm sweating in places I didn't know existed. Unless you want to conduct this meeting in the car, I don't think we need small talk."

"What do you want to know?"

"Everything."

"Come this way." Ethern lead them further into the park, over the sand dunes to a canyon buried deep within a mountain, the intricate stonework carved over eons by nature.

"This is where you were created." He knelt down and placed his hand on a burnt patch of earth glowing in the sun's rays. "It's still hot to touch after almost nine months. That was the power of your creation." Selene stepped forward and placed her on hand on the spot.

"How do you create someone like me?"

"Magic. Very powerful magic, born from Mother Nature

herself. All living multi-shifters met here and performed the ceremony. You will be involved in one, too, one day, when we need another."

"Why do you create? Can we not produce naturally?" Brayden found a spot in the shade and leaned back against the wall.

"Several male multi-shifters have bred, but their offspring take the form of their partners."

"Do you have a partner and child?"

"My work keeps me busy, so I've not had a chance."

"So, any children Brayden and I have will take the form of a snow leopard?"

"Again, on that, we can only speculate. We don't know. You are unique. The only female."

"Why was I created female? Did you choose it?"

Ethern turned away from her. "What we did was new. We didn't even know if it would work. I pleaded with the others and they accepted. All I knew is that I had to protect their hopes for you. "

"What do you mean?"

"As well as being created, you were born."

"Born? The baby in my dreams. It was me?"

"You remember?"

"A mother and father, happy. I couldn't see their faces, but I know they adored me. Then darkness and tears. An empty cot. My mother told me love is my control. The love I have for Brayden."

"Death is cruel beyond belief sometimes. He promised you would not be caused pain by this." He looked to the sky as if cursing someone. Brayden stepped forward, brought Selene into his arms, and she melted against him.

"Death came for her."

"There was nothing your parents could do. They were not magical; they were human. I'd been friends with them for several years. Your father knew of the realm in which we exist. He was a brilliant scientist and had been working with a group of volunteer shifters to try and discover more about our genetic make-up. I was one of such people. To know I was never born has always troubled me. I wanted to know more about what I truly was."

"I can relate to that."

"Thankfully, the reaper Death sent was also a friend of mine. I fear there is a lot more that exists in this world that you know off."

"I'm beginning to see that. I think I have a lot to learn."

"We'll learn it together." Brayden pulled her even tighter, and she took his hand and squeezed it.

"Why could you not ask the reaper to change Death's mind?"

"When his mind is set, it cannot be altered. The reaper allowed me time with your parents to explain the situation. They were devastated, as you can imagine. I watched your mother's heart break right there in front of me. She'd wanted a child for so long. They were an older couple. They'd not been blessed until you."

"It's just so cruel."

"It was, but I saw a way out of it. I could not stop you from dying, nobody could, but I asked for you. Death agreed."

"He agreed, just like that?"

"No. We're not immortal. Though we age more slowly than humans, we'll still die one day. When that time comes for me, I've pledged my afterlife to being a reaper. I'll walk the Earth for eternity collecting souls for Death."

"I don't understand. You did that just to have me?"

"I couldn't let the child your parents loved so much become nothing but ashes." Selene let a tear run down her cheek. Brayden moved his hand up to catch it and wipe it away.

"I'll never be able to repay you for that."

"You don't need to."

"What happened to my parents? Do they know what I am? Where I am?"

He shook his head.

"They know you live as a creation. What and where must be kept from them. That was part of Death's deal. Your father left his work after you died. He and your mother live quietly now. They mourn, but they are at peace."

"I can't see them?"

"No. You are no longer their child. The night you died, we brought your body here. It's sacred to our people. All multi-shifters are created here. The others feared the magic we were going to employ, but I managed to convince them. I'm so glad I did. You've already proven your strength and abilities."

Selene turned her head into Brayden's chest. She wept softly.

"Why can't she see them? Who said she couldn't?"

"The Council did. Selene, I know this is hard, knowing your parents are out there and within your reach. But we broke so many rules to create you. To give life to your parent's blood when they thought they had no hope. They mourn the loss of their baby, but they rejoice in the knowledge that you survive on some plane and have a purpose. The Council imposed the rules to protect everyone."

"The Council made rules I didn't consent to." She pushed off Brayden and started to make her way back through the channels of the cavern. "If I want to see my parents, I will. Nobody can stop me."

"They can, and they will."

Brayden turned and growled at Ethern. "Anyone tries to hurt her; they have to come through me." His fangs slid down.

"I'm going about this all wrong. Selene, please listen to me. It's important."

She stopped and placed her hand against a wall. Brayden opened his telepathic link to her.

"Talk to me."

"I want to see them. I want them to know that I'm alright. I hear their cries of sorrow in my head. They grieve."

"They lost a daughter. Anyone would grieve."

"But they don't have to have lost me. I'm here"

"You're not the baby they lost."

She turned back to look at him. "I'm a creation. I had no childhood. I exist only from the day I was found here."

"No." Ethern stepped up to her side. "You are wrong about what you were created for. All multi-shifters are created for helping people, but you are different. You were created for Brayden."

"What?" They both spat out.

"How can I be created for just one man. Actually, don't answer that, I'm starting to sense that this Council of yours is rather male oriented and I think the answer will be one I don't like."

"You are not created for his physical needs." Ethern looked a little red-faced.

"Although she's not bad at that." Brayden couldn't help his comment. She was, but he still received a dirty look from her for his troubles.

"There is a fight coming, one that will change the face of the Earth forever. We don't know when it will come or how it will manifest. We just know that it is coming. Brayden will be the key, and as his mate, so will you." Ethern looked up at the sky. "I must go. Research our kind, Selene. Find out all you can. And prepare. Prepare for the end."

He disappeared in a flash. For once they were both lost for words.

"I was made for you?" She ran into his arms, and he held her tight.

"Just as I was made for you." She was his reason for existing.

"I'm scared. I'm not sure I understand all of this."

"I don't think I do either. How do you feel about being specifically made for me?"

"It explains why were instantly drawn together. Why I woke up where I did and met your mother first. It shows why I only got control of my powers when I thought that I had lost you. My key, my life." Her breath was warm on his chest. "I feel scared though that I only exist because you do. I don't have an identity of my own."

"You have your own style and person in abundance. I'd never ask you just to exist for my needs." He pulled her back and cupped her face in his hands. Such a simple gesture that only a week ago would have set off her changing.

"I was made for you."

"As my partner in life, love, death, whatever comes next. Together we are strong, apart we are weak. That is why we were both made; for each other."

"I'll do whatever it takes to be your strength."

"And I yours."

"What about you? The fight? Do you think he means with Nuka?"

"Nuka will seek revenge for not having your powers. He is deluded in his own abilities and the council will see that he is destroyed for that belief."

"You don't feel that he is the fight that Ethern was talking about?"

"I believe he will be a part of it, but to play with nature as much as they have done just for him, I'm not sure. I think we need to go home and speak with Kas."

"I agree."

They made their way back to the car in silence. Just as he was about to open for the door for Selene she grabbed his hand.

"Mates?"

"Mates."

EPILOGUE

Kas stood before them, his formal suit stretched over his wide shoulders. None of the males had been happy when they'd discovered that she was going to insist on the ceremony being suited and booted. They'd had trouble finding suits for all of their broad shoulders. Made-to-measure was the way forward for shifters. Brayden looked incredibly sexy; she was already getting wet at the thought of getting back into the bedroom with him. But first, he needed to take his place as the Beta of the Glacial Blood Pack. She would be right by his side the entire time. Kas was combining the ceremony with confirmation of their mating. To all who knew them, they were in essence man and wife. She'd taken his name and proudly wore his mark upon her shoulder. For today, all fears of a future cast in shadows were put aside. The work of finding potential enemies lay unopened on Kas' desk scattered with papers. Training had ceased. Today was simply about love.

"Brayden." Kas beckoned him forward. "Do you wish to take on the role of Beta for Glacial Blood?"

"I do."

"Do you solemnly swear to honor this position? To protect those within this pack to your full abilities? Every decision that you make from this day forth will be for the pack."

"I do."

Selene looked over to Jane. The woman she now called mother had tears streaming down her face. Zain stood beside her and handed her a tissue before bringing her into a bear hug.

"Selene."

She turned back to Kas. "As Brayden's mate do you

swear to assist him in his duties forever more?"

"I do."

"Jessica?"

The witch stepped forward. She was in a beautiful teal colored gown and allowed her natural form to show, richly colored markings weaving all over her skin in intricate patterns that swirled and changed as they moved. Selene knew this was a big step for her. Generally, Jessica never showed her true self but had felt compelled to do so for the ceremony. Something dark had happened to her in the past. She hoped one day they would be friends enough to discuss it.

"You have the spell ready?" Kas enquired.

"Yes."

Brayden removed his jacket and rolled up the sleeve of his shirt. Kas groaned and rolled his eyes. The others laughed. They were one big happy family. Everyone formed a circle around them. Brayden took her hand and led her into the middle. Jessica's eyes went white, and she held her hands out in front of her. Brayden took one and Selene the other. The magic rippled through her body. Selene looked down to her bare left arm, and a marking had appeared. It marked her as the mate of the beta of the Glacial Blood Pack. She turned her attention to Brayden, who was branded with the mark of the Beta.

"It is done." Jessica couldn't help but let a massive smile wash over her face.

"Does that mean I can take my mate to the bedroom now?"

"You do realize as Beta you have to actually do some work around here?"

"Later." Brayden bent down and pulled on her lip with his teeth. "You lot can celebrate with a feast of deer. I've got another treat waiting for me."

"Brayden." Selene scowled. "Your mother is in the room."

"I think I really need to head into town later. All this sex talk is making me rather in need of a lady." Tyler cracked his neck and nodded to Scott. "You fancy joining me? I would ask Zain, but I have a feeling he'll have his head in a pot of honey in celebration."

"Always, unless... ladies?" Scott looked towards Emma, Katia and Jessica.

They all frowned at him.

"You really need to try a bit harder than that if you think you'll get into any of our pants." Katia raised an unimpressed eyebrow.

"Yeah, for example, maybe do some cooking, cleaning. That sort of thing." Emma added.

"What and risk ruining the manicure I had last week?"

"Oh, dear God." Jessica laughed.

"Actually. I would like a woman." Zain interjected. "Do you think we could find one that would let me lick honey off her?"

Everyone broke out into a fit of giggles and a lot more teasing. Selene stepped back to watch. She was home. This was her place in the world. What was coming scared them all, but together they knew they would be robust enough to fight anything.

"Welcome to the pack, Selene." Kas placed his arm around her shoulder.

"Thank you. Kas. I'm sorry for not trusting you at the start."

"That's alright. I've been told I'm difficult to warm to."

"I know that you want what's best for the pack. I'm going to help you get that. You can trust me. I know in the wrong hands I'm dangerous."

"Hush." He silenced her. "No fighting talk today. Today we celebrate." She stretched up and kissed him on the cheek. "If you want alone time with that man of yours, then I'd go and drag him away from Scott. If Brayden gets him in a headlock, then they'll be fighting all day."

She headed to collect her man, but was stopped by a flash of white light. Everyone ceased the joviality and went to fighting stance.

As the light cleared, Ethern stood in front of her with three guards.

"Ethern Lennox. What can I do for you?" Kas stepped forward and motioned for everyone to stand down.

"I'm sorry to interrupt. I'm afraid this is not a friendly visit."

"I can see that." Kas nodded towards the guards.

"Emma Bryant." Ethern turned to the lioness. The guards surrounded her. "I'm arresting you on suspicion of murder. You will come with us immediately."

THE END

GLACIAL BLOOD CONTINUES
OCTOBER/NOVEMBER 2017
FIGHTING THE LIES,
EMMA AND SCOTT'S STORY

BOOKS BY ANNA EDWARDS

Contemporary Romance:

The Control Series: A dramatic, witty, and sensual suspense romance set predominantly in London.

Surrendered Control, The Control Series, Book 1:
Amazon US http://amzn.to/2gDAgtG
Amazon UK http://amzn.to/2gGShn5
Goodreads http://bit.ly/2fOdQEK

Divided Control, The Control Series, Book 2:
Amazon US http://amzn.to/2gutKT7
Amazon UK http://amzn.to/2gDqV58
Goodreads http://bit.ly/2gdtMhv

Misguided Control, The Control Series, Book 3:
AmazonUK: http://amzn.to/2lxiqM0
Amazon US: http://amzn.to/2lxojca
Goodreads: http://bit.ly/2rEaxa5

Controlling Darkness, The Control Series, Book 4:
AmazonUK: http://amzn.eu/22w00DN
Amazon US: http://a.co/85CKiOa
Goodreads: http://bit.ly/2sr4ogP

Controlling Heritage, The Control Series, Book 5:
AmazonUK: http://amzn.eu/22w00DN
Amazon US: http://a.co/85CKiOa
Goodreads: http://bit.ly/2sr4ogP

DEAR READER

Dear Reader,

I hope you enjoyed this book. I'd love it if you could post a review about it on Amazon and Goodreads. Getting reviews for my books is such a thrill as it allows me to see what readers enjoy or even, dislike about what I write. It's all good for me to learn. Perhaps you could mention which is your favourite character and what parts you like best. You could also say which character you're looking forward to reading more about in a new book.

If you've spotted a typo, email me at <u>anna1000edwards@gmail.com</u>.

I look forward to hearing from you.

Anna Edwards

PS – Read on for a preview of CONTROLLING HERITAGE. The next book in my popular Control Series!

PREVIEW OF CONTROLLING HERITAGE

COMING 25TH JULY 2017

Sophie North is James North's little sister. She has suffered through the brutal attack on her brother all because of his sexual beliefs. This is why she now hides behind the prim and proper personal assistant who won't allow her clients to ruin themselves.

Grayson Moore, is a world famous Native American movie star. His action packed Renegade series has made him a household name and with the fame and fortune comes the reputation. He likes his alcohol strong, his cars fast and his bed full of women.

Controlling Heritage tells the story of how your upbringing can destroy your view of the world and warp it to the point where you no longer now what control is and how it should be applied.

The story features; orgies, suspense, BDSM, and lots of love. You have been warned.

Step into the world of Control!

PROLOGUE - GRAYSON

"Why don't you come here and sit on my face?" Grayson lowered his leather pants and pulled out his rigid cock; the tip already dripping with pre-cum. "And you two can suck my dick." Blonde 'one' dropped her lacy thong down her slender legs and straddled over his body and slid up to his face. He could smell how ready she was for him. It was a pretty cunt but you could tell that it got a regular fucking- but then that was what these girls were for. Brought in to satisfy his basic needs and to get off on the fact they had a movie star's dick inside them. Basic human instinct really. He was always working so didn't have a chance to find a date on his own. The woman he did meet, well he could never be sure why they wanted him for Grayson Moore the actor or person. It was a downside to the career that he loved doing.

"How do you like to be sucked, Master Grayson?" Blonde 'two' enquired while twisting her hand up his shaft.

"Show me what you know and I'll tell you if it is wrong."

He was jaded. Everyone liked to play the submissive since Fifty Shades of Grey but very few had their heart in it. He wanted a true submissive. Blonde 'Two' flicked her tongue over the tip of his cock. He wasn't as hard as he should be. That would make for good reading in the online gossip pages these girls used to discuss how good an actor was in bed. Yes, such things did exist. He better up his game and get his head on straight. The last thing he needed was to be labelled a dud in the sack.

"Take me deeper. I want to feel the back of your throat."

"I don't know if I can." She twilled in her bimbo voice. "You're so big."

"Then move aside and let your friend try. You can suck my balls instead." She pouted and her friend, blonde 'three' eagerly took over. She had his cock in her mouth and at the back of her throat in a matter of seconds. Blonde 'one' wiggled her hips against his chin. He smacked her fat injected backside.

"I say when you get off babe, not you. Spread those legs further."

She grateful obliged and he dragged his tongue up the length of her slit and drove it into her hole. Maybe he could get into this. There was nothing like a succulent pussy to make everything alright in the world. His hands slid up her body to grab a handful of her breasts. As expected they were rock hard. Un-natural.

"Fuck this." He lifted blonde 'one' up and threw her unceremoniously on the floor. Blonde 'three' paused mid-way down his dick. Her scarlet lipstick smudged over her face. "Get off me and get lost."

"What?" The sound of Blonde 'Three' reverberated around his rapidly shrinking dick.

"But your PA promised us five thousand dollars if we spent the night with you." Realising her mistake, blonde 'two' made a rapid retreat to her clothes.

"And I will pay you the same to get the FUCK out of here. Double, if you get out in the next two minutes." This time he pushed blonde 'three' off the bed and stepped over blonde 'one' who was still leg's akimbo on the floor. He yanked his jeans off a chair and put them on. A Rolling Stone's t-shirt was whipped over his head in seconds. His sneakers were next. He couldn't be bothered to tie the laces so just slid into them. Without so much as a glance over his shoulder at the naked, medically enhanced Barbie's in his luxury trailer, he slammed the door on the way out.

"Jared?" He bellowed at the top of his voice. The set was a hive of activity but everyone stopped and looked at him.

"Grayson." The slimy git of a PA appeared from up the director's arse. He was obviously butt licking again.

"You're fired." Grayson pulled back his fist and sent it flying into the shocked ex-PA's face.

ABOUT ANNA EDWARDS

Anna Edwards is a British Author that has a love of travelling and developing plot lines for stories. She has spent that last two years learning the skills of writing after being an accountant since the age of 21. As well as Roleplaying on twitter, she can also be found writing poetry on Twitter

Her debut novel, Surrendered Control was released in November 2016 and has received fantastic feedback on the drama of story. Since then she has released four other books in 'The Control Series'. The Touch of Snow is the first book in a seven (at the moment) paranormal romance series. Anna only recently discovered paranormal romance but instantly fell in love with it. Brayden and Selene's story came to her in a dream.

In her writing she loves to combine her love for romantic and erotic novels with her passion for travel to give an international feel to her novels.

Death Valley is somewhere she visited in 2008 after a tragic personal event. It was part of a tour of the west coast of America that she loved a great deal. The highlight of the trip was a helicopter ride over the Grand Canyon.

Anna Edwards likes her hero's hot and hunky with a dirty mouth. Her heroines demur but spunky and her books in a kick arse series.

CONNECT WITH ANNA EDWARDS

www.AuthorAnnaEdwards.com

Facebook, Author Page: AnnaEdwardsWriter

Facebook, Friend: TheAuthorAnnaEdwards

Twitter: @Anna__Edwards

Instagram: authorannaedwards

Pinterest: anna1000edwards

Goodreads: anna__edwards

Bookbub: https://www.bookbub.com/authors/anna-edwards

Email: anna1000edwards@gmail.com

Made in the USA
Columbia, SC
29 October 2017